SOMEDAY HER DUKE WILL COME

HAPPILY EVER AFTER BOOK 2

ELLIE ST. CLAIR

PRAIRIE LILY PRESS

Facebook: Ellie St. Clair

Cover by AJF Designs

Do you love historical romance? Receive access to a free ebook, as well as exclusive content such as giveaways, contests, freebies and advance notice of pre-orders through my mailing list!

Sign up here!

Also By Ellie St. Clair

Standalone
Unmasking a Duke
Christmastide with His Countess
Her Christmas Wish

Happily Ever After
The Duke She Wished For
Someday Her Duke Will Come
Once Upon a Duke's Dream
He's a Duke, But I Love Him
Loved by the Viscount
Because the Earl Loved Me

Happily Ever After Box Set Books 1-3
Happily Ever After Box Set Books 4-6

Searching Hearts

Duke of Christmas
Quest of Honor
Clue of Affection
Hearts of Trust
Hope of Romance
Promise of Redemption

Searching Hearts Box Set (Books 1-5)

The Unconventional Ladies
Lady of Mystery
Lady of Fortune
Lady of Providence
Lady of Charade

Blooming Brides
A Duke for Daisy
A Marquess for Marigold
An Earl for Iris
A Viscount for Violet

CONTENTS

SOMEDAY HER DUKE WILL COME

HAPPILY EVER AFTER BOOK 2

1

Matilda Andrews ducked behind another potted fern and caught her breath. Damn, that Heath Cashing was nothing if not persistent.

Her father had given the young man just enough encouragement as to his chances at winning Tillie's favor, and now he was incorrigible. He'd practically demanded a second dance earlier and it was all she could do to avoid a third before tongues really started wagging about Tillie and her second cousin.

She shuddered in disgust as she fanned herself with a gala program. She was not interested in Heath that way. In any way, actually. He was not only overbearing and obnoxious, but a bore and so preoccupied with trade rates and exchanges that every time he opened his mouth, Tillie had to force herself not to cross her eyes and fall asleep.

From her hiding place, Tillie watched the gathered crowds at the Italian Historical Society Gala. It was a fundraiser disguised as a ball and only the deepest of pockets in London had been invited—which explained her family's invitation and her father's insistence that she and her older brother Maxfield attend.

She glanced down at the olive-green ball gown she'd created for herself. The color may have washed out others, but with her warm skin tone and dark chestnut locks, it deepened the royal blue of her eyes beautifully and more than a few heads had turned her way that evening.

She figured they were admiring the gown. While Tillie may have denied her beauty, she was proud of her dress designs, and this had been one of her favorites, one she hadn't been able to part with and sell to one of the shops in town.

The wide, square neckline revealed just enough to be attractive but not suggestive, and she had designed the short puffs to rest atop sheer long sleeves underneath. The high waistline of the dress flowed down to a skirt that flared in the back, showcasing her feminine form.

Poor Max. There were scores of things her bookwormish older brother would rather be doing than chaperoning his little sister at yet another dance, but there he was, holding the most awkward of conversations with a country curate who'd also found himself invited.

Tillie kept moving, weaving in and out of the mass of bodies who were trying to get closer to the guests of honor seated on a dais at the front of the massive hall. Count Campagna and his wife were politely listening to the overlong stories told by the society's president, a local baron with loads of money and a wife with a love of opera.

At her very core, Tillie was a student of fashion. She designed dresses and sewed samples, which she provided to the finer dress shops in Cheapside. More than a few collaborations had been struck that way.

It was because of her ability to not only design a

gorgeous dress that caught the eye, but to also convince fashion houses to take a chance on her that meant a large number of young debutantes each season wore a gown that Matilda Andrews had designed.

Most of them, however, weren't aware that the designer of their dresses was the daughter of the shipping magnate Baxter Andrews. She did all she could to keep her two lives separate, wanting to make her own way in the design world.

Tillie herself was not a debutante. Despite the assumption of most that every young lady of eligible age wanted to be primped and prepared like some stuffed doll waiting to be picked as a prize, she wasn't much interested in being put on display like a mannequin in the dress shops. No, what Tillie wanted more than anything else was the freedom to be whoever it was she chose to be.

She squinted, trying her best to get a look at what the countess was wearing. Was fashion ahead or behind London in Rome? She stepped sideways as a short, round man told a rousing tale about hunting and nearly bashed the side of her head with his champagne glass. As it was, liquid sloshed out of the glass, splashing on her face. She blinked as the bubbly alcohol stung her eye.

Tillie squeezed her eyes shut against the irritation of it and put her hands out in front of her as she tried to walk back toward the refreshments room. Was she even going the right way? She prayed to the gods of party etiquette that she didn't knock over a priceless marble statue on her blind and fumbling way to find a napkin somewhere.

It took her a while, but eventually she found her way into the room with the long buffet table and settings of food and drinks. Trying to hold herself together long enough to dab at her eyes with something dry, she smiled lamely at people who tried to make small talk and continued her search.

At last. In the farthest corner of the room, she finally found the linen squares neatly folded and all but hidden from view. It figured.

As she turned toward the corner and dabbed at her eyes, slowly restoring her vision, she laughed softly to herself and thought about the laugh her best friend Tabitha would have enjoyed at the debacle she'd narrowly avoided.

She would be certain to include it in the next letter she penned to the traveling Duchess of Stowe, who was currently in Paris with her Duke of a husband and her plum of a new life. Hers was a fairy tale story with an incredibly happy ending that Tillie was grateful for. It had been a rough few years for Tabitha since her father had died. Wild ups and downs constituted her whirlwind courtship with Nicholas, but it ended happily ever after.

It was a beautiful love story that was still unfolding, but it belonged to Tabitha. Tillie swallowed hard at the prospect of her own love story including a man like Heath Cashing in the role of hero and she shuddered.

No — just, no.

As if summoned by her very thoughts, she noticed that Heath had come through the doors that led to the dance floor, his eyes scanning the faces in the room. Searching for her, naturally. Tillie had managed to avoid him for nearly three dances and she knew he'd be more insistent soon. Turning quickly, she ducked into the crowd and kept her face lowered as she attempted to look both natural and invisible. It was a delicate balance she was going for, but when she found herself pushing through the second set of doors that led to another part of the dance floor, Tillie felt almost victorious.

In the span of a quarter hour, she'd not only managed to commit a new dress neckline to memory (thanks to the Italian countess) but she'd also, so far, dodged another stifling, foot-numbing turn about the floor with Cashing.

"Not so bad, old girl," she whispered to herself. "Still light on your feet when it really counts."

Casting another glance over her shoulder, she instantly deflated when she saw that Cashing was hot on her trail once more—he'd even caught sight of her and was awkwardly calling after her as she moved.

Tillie rolled her eyes and groaned under her breath, pretending not to hear him as she looked for another avenue. Surely there was somewhere she could escape to that Cashing couldn't follow?

In desperation, she turned her eyes to the dance floor. Perhaps she could quickly find herself a new dance partner? Everywhere she looked, however, dancers were already coupled.

"Miss Andrews," a deep, rich voice, perhaps from Heaven itself and most definitely not belonging to Heath Cashing, came from her left. She turned sharply and nearly smashed her face into a broad chest sporting a fine black suit. Craning her neck up, she instantly recognized the very handsome, very rakish smile of Alexander Landon, newly minted Duke of Barre.

He was the best friend and cousin of Tabitha's husband Nicholas, and Tillie had spent a charming few days flirting with the Duke during the couple's wedding festivities. She'd nearly gotten lost in his easy smiles and charming lines, but when the couple had left for their honeymoon, Tillie forced herself to come down from the fantasy she'd been living in and return to her world—the real world, where she was the daughter of a rich shipping merchant and he was a peer. A peer who charmed his way through a long line of women.

Tillie had been proud of herself for showing such resolve, too, and had assumed that she was all but over her little crush.

That was until she found herself nose to chest with the very same man.

It had been six months since she'd last seen Alexander and he was still just as gorgeous as ever. He stood well over six-feet tall with blond hair pomaded nicely off his face, despite a few strands that fell just over his forehead in an appealing way that never failed to catch her eye. His eyes were a brilliant blue, and from the look of the few adorable freckles that dotted his nose, Alexander had spent his time this summer in the sun.

It suited him, Tillie thought to herself.

"Your Grace," Tillie said with a dip of her head, her cheeks flushing and her throat constricting. If he noticed her quick reaction to him, Alexander didn't make it obvious. Without meaning to, Tillie shot a nervous look over her shoulder and saw that Heath was getting closer. Turning back to Alexander, she didn't miss the predatory smile on his face.

"None of that 'Your Grace' with me," he said. "I feel we know one another better than that. You're in need of a white knight right now, aren't you, milady?" The grin that stretched across his handsome features was magnetic and she couldn't help but give a laugh before remembering Cashing was coming.

"Actually," she said as she swallowed, "I seem to be."

"Dance with me?" Alexander offered her his arm and before she could think twice, she took it. Heads turned their way, as they made a striking couple. Tillie's hair, as dark as Alexander's was blond, was swept up away from her face into an intricate knot on her head, tendrils of curls framing her face. Her eyes were so blue they were almost violet, her mouth a perfect bow that was now turned up in its natural smile.

As he led her to the dance floor, Alexander's voice was right next to her ear, sending a shiver across her neck and down her shoulders.

"I'm glad I found you, Miss Andrews. I've been hoping to cross paths with you these past few weeks," he said in a low voice as he steered her closer to the assembling dancers. She looked at him with a question on her face. He'd been hoping to run into her?

"Why might that be?"

"Because," he said as his warm fingers wrapped around her elbow, just before he released her to her spot in the line of dancers. "I have a proposition for you. One that will help us both out of a precarious position."

With that, he gave a pointed look over her shoulder. Turning to follow his gaze, Tillie saw Cashing standing on the edge of the floor, arms folded over his chest and a frown pasted on his face.

Tillie turned back to Alexander, but before she could question him, the dance began and she found herself moving in the opposite direction.

Damn.

As the dance progressed, she realized she was going to be doing a turn or two with Alexander. Perhaps he'd explain himself a little. When they connected and he held her elbow, he gave her a grin.

"Do you remember what you said to me the last time we spoke?"

She gave him a quizzical look, but he turned and danced with the partner to her left, as prompted.

The last time they spoke? It was at Tabitha and Nicholas' wedding, but nothing much stood out. He'd been a flirt, for sure, but Tillie had known better than to fall under the young peer's charming spell. No, she'd read too many novels about what happened to common girls who put their futures in the hands of wealthy, self-absorbed aristocrats and she had no desire to end up like one of those tragic heroines, who only learn their lessons moments before some gruesome death that usually involved childbirth and a baby out of matrimony.

Tillie shuddered at the thought. Dukes were to be avoided and Tabitha's luck had been merely a fluke.

She neared Alexander again.

"Well?" He raised an eyebrow.

"We said a great many things, Your Grace," she said quickly, before they had to change partners again. "You more than most, and yet none of them seem to be very unforgettable. Pray refresh my memory?"

He gave her a very brief, very fake pained expression before schooling his features as he began dancing with the lady to her right.

"You wound me, Miss Andrews," he said over his shoulder before continuing the dance with his new partner.

Tillie gave an unladylike snort and quickly shook her head to hide it when her own new partner looked affronted at the dismissive noise.

"Terribly sorry," she said quickly. "Dust in the air, I believe."

Appeased, they continued the dance with no additional near breaches in polite society etiquette. Tillie had to stop herself from rolling her eyes at the very notion. These upper crusts were the epitome of savages when it came to the games they played with one another over fortunes, marriages, and reputations.

Polite society, indeed.

"You told me that you had no interest in marrying a duke. Or any other aristocrat for that matter," Alexander's low voice was back and he was directly behind her. The combination of the two sent a shiver down her spine. "You called aristocrats shallow and vapid, I believe. Present company included, were your words."

They turned and faced the far wall and she took the chance to look up into his intense gaze.

"If I may be so bold, I'd like a chance to explain to you that an engagement to a duke could be a very good thing for you and your career."

2

Tillie's eyes widened as she took him in. He seemed to be quite serious and her curiosity got the better of her.

Before they could be swept up in another dance, and before Cashing could find her, she discreetly pulled on the Duke's arm and steered him toward the large double doors that led to a veranda overlooking the gardens.

Blessedly, the space was empty, but Tillie moved them to a quiet corner between two giant potted ferns, lest prying eyes or a desperate Heath Cashing should try to find them.

"So forward," the Duke smirked as she pulled him into the secluded spot. "We are not even engaged yet, Miss Andrews. Whatever will the people think of the two of us?"

He was teasing her, that much was obvious by the dancing light in his eyes.

"What are you going on about — an engagement to a duke?" Tillie asked him, her brow furrowed in confusion. "Are you up to your old tricks again? Is this some kind of ploy?"

Tabitha had relayed a series of stories over the months

about Alexander's past indiscretions. Nothing so smarmy as abandoned heiresses across London, but he was known as a bit of a rake who had done outlandish things like carousing and gambling just to get under his late father's skin.

Alexander scowled at the question.

"Wait," he said, cocking his head to one side. "You know about the good old days?"

She closed her eyes and shook her head.

"I've heard stories," she said, her patience being tested. She didn't have time for a silly duke and the many ways he contrived to get under his family's skin and into women's hearts and beds. "And I am not interested in whatever game you are playing. I have plenty of my own issues to worry about."

She made a move to go, but his arm shot out and trapped her. She looked from the fine sleeve of his charcoal jacket and up to his face, challenging him. His eyes pleaded with her to listen for a moment.

"In my defense, I was a young man in desperate need of my father's attentions, and the stories have been greatly exaggerated," he said, serious now. "However, that is not what this is about. I truly have been looking for you in earnest — I have a situation arising that I need help with and I believe I can equally be of service to you."

He lowered his arm and she crossed hers over her chest. She was not exactly running away, but was still not trusting what the man was about quite yet.

"I did a little listening around the markets and business district in an attempt to find you, little wraith that you are," he said. "Talk of the wharves is that your father is pressuring you to marry someone specific. Someone that you have rebuffed time and again."

Cashing. She made a bitter face at the name alone,

which Alexander caught. He had met the man on occasion and could understand her avoidance.

"Such a bad chap?"

She rolled her eyes. She wasn't going to play his word games just yet.

"Keep going," she warned. "We have been out here long enough. Tongues are going to start to wag if you are not careful."

The amusement was back in his eyes and he dared a wink at her.

"Something tells me you do not care a lick what the old marms and gossips have to say, do you?"

She sucked in a breath—of course she didn't. But she had five unmarried brothers and a father with business interests throughout England. She didn't want to cause her family any harm because of a silly conversation with a handsome duke.

"Your Grace —,"

"Alexander."

"Your Grace... Alexander," she ground out, giving him her best glare. "You need to tell me what you're about now or I am walking away and not looking back."

He looked up into the garden then, his eyes far away and if she wasn't mistaken, she saw the glow from a small ember of pain. His lips thinned and he blinked slowly.

"I was in love once," he began, completely shocking her with a frank admission and the fact that he was no longer jesting. "She broke my heart and left me completely bereft and it has taken me almost two years to come to terms with it—to know that my behavior, as obnoxious as it is, is just a balm to soothe the ache that still festers sometimes."

Tillie held her breath at the confession. Where had this come from?

"She moved into another circle and had suitors falling at her feet, one duke in particular who is much grander than I could ever be," he said. "But there are circumstances in the coming months that will put us in the same parties and affairs once again."

She waited. What did this have to do with her?

As if reading her mind, he continued.

"And that is where you come in," he said. "I do not trust myself to not fall into her traps again, to be a fool for her once more. And this time, I have a lot more to lose as the head of my family and properties. I need a bolster. A partner who will serve as a barrier between myself and this woman."

She frowned.

"I am sorry, Your Grace," she began, trying her best not to belittle his feelings. "But that sounds ridiculous. Having an imposter beside you will not stop your feelings from resurfacing or returning. Only you can do that, yourself, through time and effort."

He closed his eyes and raked his hand through his hair, disheveling it in the most charming way, Tillie caught herself noticing.

"I have tried," he said miserably, "and failed. And now that I have a lot more at stake, I cannot allow myself to act rashly or make mistakes that could cost my family and the families who depend on us. Do you not see? If she gets back into my head and manipulates me once more, I would sell the shirt off my back to keep her happy. I need your help for a few short months — weeks even. That is all. Help me get through the next season of parties and then we will both be free to go our separate ways."

Tillie sucked in a breath.

"And the shame that comes from a broken engagement? Even a false one?"

It was definitely something worth considering on both their parts, though Tillie wasn't interested in marriage to begin with. Still, it had the potential to bring embarrassment to her family and that was something to keep in mind. Her father's business had provided her family with comforts and social status that her mother and siblings thrived on. Any rash act on her part that jeopardized that would give her cause to reconsider.

"If you understood the pain I have had to endure at Eliza's betrayal, a few simple rumors would seem like nothing to you, too," he said quietly. "And as for yourself, I think that breaking off an engagement with a wealthy duke would only add to the mystery and allure around the life you are creating. But that is just a self-serving hunch I have."

Self-serving, indeed. Men, especially handsome, wealthy ones, tended to have thick, protective armor around their reputations while less wealthy, more common women did not.

"I am still not grasping your ends out of this," Tillie said slowly, her mind racing to fully comprehend what was being offered and what was at stake. "What are you after? To make this woman jealous? To make her regret breaking your heart?"

His look grew distant again and it was a few moments before he spoke.

"My heart needs a shield, I suppose," he said. "I am going to have to face Eliza, frequently, in the upcoming weeks and you can call me a coward if you like, but I need an ally. I need someone who will remind me to be brave and keep my eyes forward—never backward to what might have been and who she might have been to me."

Her heart softened at the pained words. He was well and truly hurting—even after nearly two years, it seemed.

Tillie herself had never fallen so deeply for another that her entire happiness and wellness were at their mercy. She shuddered against the thought, actually. That would be a living hell for her—to love another so deeply and fully that the slightest misstep could send your entire world up in flames.

No, thank you.

"And you would be paid handsomely, I assure you," he said quickly, his face lighting up and covering the pain that had been there just moments before. "Not that I assume you need it, but a businesswoman like yourself could probably always use more capital."

It was true. She *could* use more money for better supplies and tools. If the price were enough, she could even set herself up with her own studio somewhere, critics be damned. The thought of an open, airy space just for her and her designs sent a little thrill through her. It would be a dream come true...

"Already counting the coins, are we?" Alexander was teasing her, having caught Tillie's dreamy expression.

"Measuring the floor space of my dream studio, actually," she admitted a little sheepishly. "Although I would implore you, Your Grace, to please keep my business activities somewhat quiet. Many aren't approving of my chosen profession." She sucked in a breath and then held it while her thoughts raced and Alexander continued to look at her with a question on his face. She chewed her lip.

"Why me, Your Grace?" she asked quickly, before she lost her nerve. While she'd definitely felt a spark blaze between them during the events that surrounded Tabitha and Nicholas' nuptials, she'd never deluded herself into thinking it was anything more than casual flirting on his part. "There must be a hundred girls across London alone who would eat their own hat for a chance to be your fiancée — even a fake one."

He shook his head a little sadly.

"Believe it or not, you are wrong," he said quietly. "I am not quite the Casanova you think me to be and I do not spend my days chasing bubble-headed girls. I have never been interested in that. And you, Miss Andrews, are the perfect woman for the job. You see through my impenetrable charm – I realized this during the wedding festivities. You are also intelligent and I can trust that you will not fall madly in love with my money or my title. No, I think you are the only person for the job."

She considered his words. No, she wasn't impressed by titles or wealth, although the Duke himself did have the propensity to send her heart aflutter. She was also still uncertain about the repercussions for both of them not only due to a broken engagement, but also if the ruse were uncovered. It could all be disastrous.

Then again, it could mean the cementing of the freedom that she'd been working so hard for these past years. In one short holiday season, she could rid herself of the financial worry that accompanies women of a certain age who have no desire to chase fortunes or play coy hostess to the suitors her father drummed up from the dregs of bachelorhood.

The situation could either be nirvana or disaster and at this exact moment, Tillie couldn't be certain.

"I need to think on it," she said quietly, looking up to meet his eyes. She saw hope and a tinge of resignation in them. Poor soul. Still, it wasn't a decision to be taken lightly and wagging purse strings in front of her face wasn't going to sway her into a poor decision. "I shall give you an answer within the week."

Relief washed over the Duke's face.

"I am staying at my mother's apartments on Henley Street, Miss Andrews," he said with a bow, casting his eyes over his shoulder. He was going to disappear first, giving her room to return to the party and find her brother. "Send word when you have agreed."

"I have not promised anything yet—" she began, but he was off before she could finish, vaulting over the railing and taking off into the cool darkness of the garden.

3

Alexander sauntered along the dark garden path with a smile on his lips. He knew in his heart that Tillie would eventually agree to his plan. As much as she tried to hide the fact that she was the face behind her designs, he knew all about her work from Nicholas and Tabitha.

He was not completely up to date on women's fashions, but if the dress she wore tonight was one of her own designs, he knew she was talented. A woman like her, who was determined to create for herself the future she had always envisioned, would stop at nothing to achieve it.

Clearly that future did not include a man like Heath Cashing. The man was deplorable and he could see why Tillie was avoiding him. Alexander, however, knew he should be thankful to Cashing for running Tillie into his arms.

Alexander had been quite stricken by Tillie Andrews during the nuptials of Nicholas, his friend and cousin, who married Tillie's best friend, Tabitha. True, most men were captured by Tillie's beauty, but it was more than that. She was her own woman, something that was difficult to find, particularly among the peerage he typically associated with.

He had tried to win her over, but it seemed she had quite the wrong impression of him. Perhaps, he admitted to himself, there was more than a bit of truth to what she had assumed, that he was a rake with a string of women left in his wake, but it was not quite that way. He loved to flirt and was drawn to beautiful women, but he certainly didn't take advantage of them the way some liked to believe.

He had been dismayed when Tillie had rebuked his advances, and now he hoped he could convince her that he wasn't the man she thought he was.

Perhaps he hadn't needed to establish such an elaborate story for her. He knew, however, she would see through most schemes. This particular plot to win her over was based on truth. He *had* been enamored with Eliza Masters, and she *had* dumped him for another. The Masters were also scheduled to visit his family home this holiday season, and he was not looking forward to seeing her again, particularly now that she was apparently all but engaged to another man, while he was quite alone. He had been somewhat grief stricken for a time, it was true; however, unlike what he told Tillie, he figured he was intelligent enough not to fall for her ploys again.

That Tillie Andrews could be on his arm through the parties of the season was an idea that had come to him when he saw her across the room at the gala. He felt he needed to give her a purpose in order to convince her to come, and thus he hastily formulated the plan. He thought the idea quite inspired, and now he could only wait until she agreed to accompany him.

He had left the ball after jumping into the garden greenery, not having much interest in anyone there beyond Tillie Andrews.

He rose early the next morning, and was pleasantly surprised to find his mother joining him at the breakfast table. She typically took breakfast in her rooms, but he wanted to speak to her today about his plans.

Leticia Landon was not a typical member of the *ton*. She was beautiful, polished, and refined, but she also saw through people and preferred to get to the heart of the matter, saying what she thought rather than speak in circles as others did. Alexander appreciated that about her, and had always spoken rather plainly with her. He wasn't sure if she would approve of his scheming, but he knew he could convince her to go along with it. As Alexander was her only child, she was wont to give into what he asked of her.

"Mother," Alexander greeted her, as he rose and kissed her on the cheek, pulling her chair out to seat her. "You look radiant this morning, as always."

She eyed him warily. "And what would you be wanting from me today, Alex, dear?"

"Why should I want something?"

"You only compliment me so eloquently when there is something you need."

"I do not see any issue in telling my mother how beautiful she is," he said, sitting down and pouring both of them a cup of tea. He reached across the table for a piece of toast, which he buttered as he glanced over at her. "There is a matter you may be interested in, however," he said.

"Yes?" Her eyebrows raised expectantly.

"Do you recall the young woman who stood up for Tabitha at her wedding to Nicholas?"

"Of course," his mother replied. "She was quite striking. In fact, I recall you seemed to be somewhat taken with her."

"I was," he said. "In fact, I still am. I saw her again at the Italian Historical Society Gala."

"Correct me if I am wrong, but is she not the daughter of a shipping man without title?"

"No title, Mother, and that adds to her appeal," he said. "I am finished with the *ton*."

"After your experience with Eliza Masters?" she asked, sipping her own tea, her toast barely touched on the plate in front of her.

"Interesting you should bring up Eliza, Mother," said Alexander, before launching into the scheme he had proposed to Tillie. "When she agrees, and I know she will, I need your help."

"Alexander, this is all rather preposterous," she said. "Why do you not just ask to court the girl? Any woman — particularly a common woman — would feel quite fortunate to have a man such as yourself interested in her."

"Tillie is not as common as she seems, and she seems to have some misgivings about my... reputation," he said. "I need her to come to know me, the true Alexander Landon. That is what I need your help with. I would like her to join us for the holiday season at Warfield Manor. It would not be seemly for me to ask her directly, so I should like you to ask her, if you would."

Leticia shook her head at her son and his plotting. He had taken the situation with Eliza quite badly last year, though he seemed to have recovered. She had known the girl since she was a child, and found her to be callous and calculating. She was a woman who knew her appeal to men, and used it to her advantage. Once she had tossed Alexander over, Leticia could no longer stand the girl at all, but her father had been a good friend of her departed husband. She had not understood how her son had been so taken with his daughter. Yes, she had her looks, but could he not see how she manipulated him? The girl's mother had been the same in her youth, if Leticia recalled correctly.

She looked at Alexander and made up her mind. She would go along with the scheme, if for no other reason than she wanted to see the look on Eliza Master's face when she saw Alexander with a beautiful fiancée on his arm.

"Yes, Alexander," she said with a nod. "I agree to your scheme. What do we do next?"

"Next?" he said, grinning at his mother. "We wait."

4

Tillie had asked for a week to make up her mind, but it didn't take a week. In fact, it didn't even take 72 hours for her to arrive at the conclusion that if she didn't do something to take control of her own destiny right now, she'd end up the bored, nameless housewife of a man such as Heath Cashing.

The Andrews family, with the exception of Stephen and Ethan, her two married brothers, were just finishing a large Sunday breakfast together after the siblings had gone to church. Her parents seldom accompanied them, but as long as the children attended, they considered their appearances sufficiently "kept up."

Tillie, the only daughter of the Andrews' eight children, was always required to attend as she generated the most conversation — what she wore, who she spoke with. The mothers in the crowd were, of course, interested in her brothers, particularly the older ones, but two were now attached and the rest currently occupied with their own occupations.

"Heath said you and Max disappeared from the gala early last night," her father Baxter said, his giant mustache dripping with eggs and coffee. Really, her father was a good man. He was. But he was also blessedly out of touch with a lot of things — common decorum and his daughter's most heartfelt desires in life chief among them.

Max's eyes jumped up to Tillie's from his round spectacles, the look of panic clear. As the most quiet and reserved member of the family, the last thing he wanted was to be in the crosshairs of their loud, rambunctious father, lest he get any ideas of matrimony and matchmaking for him, as he did for Tillie. Sensing her brother's panic, Tillie jumped in.

"I grew tired of dancing, Papa," she said sweetly. Baxter was a shrewd businessman, but he was also an absolute sucker when it came to the fairer sex. A few batted eyelashes and a puckered pout and he was putty.

"Poor child," he said with a grin. "It's a shame you were born so beautiful, was it not? I blame your mother. You certainly did not get your looks from me."

He chuckled at himself. It was true. His wife, Gloria, was stunning, even in her 50s. She was elegant and refined and perfectly happy in the role her husband had given her. On the darker nights, Tillie sometimes wished she could just give up her dreams of creativity and freedom and settle into a placid domestic role (and *enjoy* it) like her mother did. It would make life so much simpler.

But the bottom line and the ugly truth were quite clear to Matilda Olive Andrews — she wasn't her mother and never would be. And what could she ever have in common with the woman who had agreed to give her daughter a middle name in honor of the import that had made them the most money the year of her birth? She shook her head against the very notion of being named after an olive.

"I am quite certain Mr. Cashing was able to carry on and find other amusements in our absence," she said, hoping the matter would be put to rest.

"He was certainly upset," Baxter continued, *not* dropping it no matter how much Tillie wished he would. "Told me all about it the next morning in the tariff office. Said he was worried you had come down with an illness and wanted to make sure you were well."

Tillie could hardly control the roll of her eyes and reined them in at the very last second. Heath Cashing certainly didn't care about her or her well being. If he did, he would stop pursuing her like she was some sort of prey with a very large bounty attached to it.

"Well, I am perfectly fine. And I am sure Mr. Cashing is quite well, himself," she said quickly. "There is no need to worry the situation further." She *really* wanted to stop talking about Cashing.

"Matilda," her father said, his tone changing. She immediately looked to him, knowing something was amiss. He was loud and boisterous and to have his tone suddenly go soft and serious meant there was likely bad news following.

"Yes, Papa?"

He closed his eyes and took the moment to wipe the bits of breakfast from his face.

"I had a visit with my physician yesterday, child, because of the bouts of shortness of breath I have been experiencing lately. He did not exactly provide me with the most optimistic outlook," he said. The chatter amongst her brothers stopped and all eyes were suddenly turned to Baxter. "It seems I have some trouble with my heart, and therefore the physician is unsure what the future might hold for me."

Her eyes shot to her mother, who had her head bowed

and wouldn't look up. The information wasn't new to her, apparently.

"Whatever do you mean?" Tillie asked, despite the fact that she was quite intelligent and knew exactly what he was implying. He was sick.

"Nobody is promised another day, Matilda," her father said solemnly. "It is my new mission to see you happy and well taken care of. Married, Tillie. It is my wish that you get married to a respectable man. Can I say that any more plainly?"

"Papa," she said quietly, "I am so sorry to hear you are ill. You know how much I love you. If you take care of yourself, I am sure we can keep you healthy, isn't that right Mamma?"

Her mother nodded her assent, and her brothers chimed in as well. They would all do what they could for their father.

"So you understand now how important it is to find a husband for you?"

Despite the sobering news, she didn't appreciate her father using his health as a bargaining chip. She chose her words carefully. Her father, jovial as he was, also had a temper. She typically didn't back down, but he could win any argument when his anger raged like a sea storm.

Besides that, she was deeply concerned for his health and that mattered more than anything at the moment. "I do want to see you happy, Papa," she continued, "but I am not marrying Heath Cashing."

She heard her mother's gasp and at least two of her brothers inched away from the table, preparing for impact.

Surprisingly, her father didn't blow up.

"Then who, child?"

She chewed her lower lip.

"I do not want to get married," she said, her voice shaking a bit. She was speaking the truth, but she was also breaking every social and family norm in the books. It was simply unheard of for a perfectly sane, moderately wealthy young woman from an up-and-coming family not to make a good match.

Her father closed his eyes, his ruddy cheeks reddening even darker now.

"Love," her mother's voice came from the far side of the table, calm and gentle. "Perhaps you should go lie down. Calm yourself a bit. We will not solve all of our problems in one day, you know."

Her father's dark eyes went from Tillie to her mother and back again and despite the nod that followed, the warning look he sent Tillie let her know the conversation would continue. And, from the glare her mother shot her way as they left the table, there would be consequences for her actions that morning.

IT TOOK a whole day for the repercussions to become clear.

Tillie was putting on her coat and jacket to head to Downey's, as they had asked to see a few of her holiday gown designs. Their housekeeper Helene stopped her before she could leave.

"You're wanted upstairs in your mother's sitting room, Miss," Helene said, standing in front of the door. The sitting room was her mother's realm. Her mother never wanted Tillie up there, her personal tastes and activities so different than Tillie's. This wasn't good.

Slowly taking the steps, Tillie rounded the corner and

walked down toward her mother's sitting room with trepidation. It was a small, pleasant room that overlooked the garden in the back of the house. It was where her mother commonly did what Tillie referred to as "Matron of the Home" duties. She didn't want to think of the hours her mother and her female servant spent in this tiny space, mending ripped trousers and cleaning stained curtains. It made Tillie's skin itch just thinking about all that time spent nattering away.

"You sent for me, Mamma?" she asked as she pushed the door open.

Her mother was bent over a linen, repairing a slight rip in it. At her feet was a basket with what looked to be a pile of her brothers' trousers. Tillie involuntarily winced.

"There are six pairs of trousers that need holes mended and two tablecloths that need stains removed," her mother said, motioning toward the basket with the hand that held the needle.

Tillie looked blankly from the pile back to her mother and frowned.

"I have plans, Mamma," she said with a vague motion of her arm toward the front door downstairs. "I shall be late if I do not leave now."

Her mother set the piece that she was working on down on her lap and looked up, finally meeting her daughter's eyes.

"Your days of traipsing to and fro across the city with nary a care in the world are quite done, Matilda," she said flatly, ignoring the fact that Tillie's mouth dropped open. "We all have to do our duties to this family and it seems you are the only one who feels she is exempt. Well, you are not. From today forward you will help Helene with whatever repairs are necessary and then you will help Cook with dinner in the kitchens."

"You are making me a servant in this house because I refuse to marry Heath Cashing?" Her voice was pitchy by now but Tillie didn't care who heard.

"So, do not marry Heath Cashing, though I dare say you could hardly do better than a solid man with a good profession to provide for you," her mother said as she put the work on the chair beside her. "But you are no longer going to carry on like a wild thing that you have been, utilizing your father's resources to do heaven knows what throughout London. I am going to teach you to run the household, as you shall have to do when you marry. You will do it with your hands in the soapy water and fingers on the needles."

Tillie couldn't breathe. She couldn't move. More than anything, she wanted to think that her mother was jesting. Her whole life her mother knew she'd had little to zero interest in the day-to-day duties she contended with. Tillie thought her mother understood her need for creativity and freedom. Never before had there been an issue of her leaving the house when she wished, planning her own schedule. She had always felt fortunate to be afforded nearly the same freedoms as her brothers.

Had she been mistaken this entire time?

"Your father has been lax with you and now he is not in a position to fight with you about marriage and moving out to establish and raise your own family," her mother said as she advanced on Tillie. "But I can. And I will. Starting today, you will do what I say, when I say it. Unless you want to rethink your 'no marriage' mindset?"

Checkmate.

Her mother was a shrewd tactician and she'd cornered Tillie with the choices she left her. Biting her lip, Tillie turned on her heel and marched down the hallway to her room, ripping open the desk drawer as she flopped down onto the chair.

She scrawled a hasty note and asked her trusted maid Annie to have her brother Thompson deliver it to Henley Street.

Her mother might have moves, but she didn't count on Tillie to have a few of her own.

The afternoon passed slowly and toward the end of the day, after she'd helped Cook peel at least two-dozen half-moldy potatoes, she worried that her note had either been lost or intercepted.

"Looks like we shall be seeing more of your pretty face down here, eh, Miss Andrews?" The large, middle-aged cook with chin hairs teased her.

"Not likely," Tillie said miserably. The house staff were good people and she usually got on well with them all, but they were enjoying her new role a little too much for her tastes.

For the entire rest of the day, Tillie worked. She knew that there was no way around it until her note was received and her plan put into action in the form of Alexander Landon. By the time supper had arrived, she wasn't certain that her white knight was coming at all.

Had he changed his mind? Was he punishing her for taking three days to decide?

She rubbed her aching wrist and began compiling a list of torture methods she would like to employ on the Duke if he didn't play his role soon. Another day of labor at the hands of her mother would surely do her in. She had newfound respect for the servants.

She'd never been afforded the chance to work on the ships like her brothers had. Three had taken to it, the rest had not and that was fine with their parents as long as they found respectable professions. Why was marriage the only option for her? Why wasn't she afforded the same chance to choose something other than the obvious as long as she found herself respectable work? She'd already done that part — her dresses were among the most popular in the city each season.

She'd once attempted to talk to her mother about the success of her designs, but she'd been silenced just a few words in.

"Hand me that basket of buttons, will you, Tillie?" her mother had asked without looking up. She'd tried just once more and met the same reaction — effectively ending her desire to include her mother in her seamstress and design work. When she'd tried to speak to her father about it, he told her affectionately how glad he was that she had found a hobby.

She needed a long-term plan, but she required time to put it into action. This charade with Alexander would keep her parents at bay while also providing her with additional start-up funding. Between that and money she had saved from sales thus far, she figured she could venture out on her own, no longer reliant on her family's wealth to keep her afloat. True, she would no longer live as she was accustomed, but she would be free, and that was what mattered.

As the potatoes she'd peeled were served by one of their staff at the supper table that evening, her mother took great care in describing Tillie's activities that day in detail. She glared at the obligatory snickers from her younger brothers, received the nod of approval from the two oldest, and an ear-to-ear grin from her father. She could only bite down her disappointment as she swallowed the suddenly chalky, unpalatable potatoes. If only her father would be as happy for her to be doing work she loved, as he was with her brothers.

She glanced out the window at the setting sun and fumed before stabbing another bite of her dinner. Prince Charming was taking his sweet time in setting her fairy tale into motion.

5

Up and moving before her mother rose, Tillie hit the door like the hem of her pretty pink walking dress was on fire. Her brother Ambrose was headed into Cheapside to exchange a few notes of currency before he set sail to India after the holidays, so Tillie demanded that he let her accompany him.

"I am picking up a few things for Mamma's sewing basket."

The lie slipped so easily from her tongue she was almost ashamed. Almost. Her mother had cast the die and now it was up to Tillie to keep the game in play, even if it meant fibbing to poor, unsuspecting Ambrose a bit. He was a good brother and once he'd been convinced, he went back to his plans for India, which had previously been holding his attention.

They parted ways at the currency office and she set off on foot for the dress shop. She knew she'd made a bad impression yesterday by missing her appointment, but hopefully the shop manager would be understanding and forgiving. She prayed he would, anyway. You never knew what to expect. The last appointment she had been late for at another shop resulted in a small Austrian owner greeting her with only a bad temper and a penchant for pointing a finger at her chest.

Ambrose wasn't comfortable leaving Tillie to walk the two blocks alone, but she convinced him to come collect her when he was done, meaning she'd only be walking alone one way. Hardly worth any fuss, really, and because she pouted and gave him her innocent face (Ambrose was his father's son, after all), he sighed and simply nodded, telling her he'd be there to collect her in a quarter hour at most.

It didn't give her much time, but she was determined to make the best use of it to apologize and plead her case to schedule a second appointment.

She wove in and out of the crowd headed in what felt like the opposite direction of the mass of people before she finally had the building in sight, down at the far end of the street. It was relatively quiet looking from the outside, no rush of people milling around trying to get fitted. She knew it was a specialty shop, and she hoped her designs would do well there.

Tillie straightened her dress, righted the hat on her head, and pulled her pelisse tighter around her shoulders, the London air nipping at her cheeks as winter was rolling in. She began making her way toward the shop, when she heard a very familiar, very nasally voice from a few steps back.

"Miss Andrews! Is that you? Miss Andrews? Pardon me, sir..."

Clamping her mouth down to keep herself from cursing aloud in frustration, Tillie quickly shot forward into the crowd to try to lose Cashing before he got any closer.

Tillie was small and agile, having spent years roughhousing with her brothers against the loud protests of their mother, who found the entire thing unladylike and taxing on her nerves.

In and out she wove, hoping to hear the sound of Heath Cashing fading as he struggled to weave and dance through the crowd like she was. At last, she neared the shop and glanced over her shoulder, not seeing him in the crowd on the sidewalk. She'd lost him, she thought triumphantly.

She was reaching for the door handle when his voice was behind her once more.

"There you are! Did you not hear me? I have been calling to you for the past block and a half, Miss Andrews!"

Forcing herself away from the door, she turned to him and met his eyes, forcing a tight smile on her face.

"Good morning, Mr. Cashing," she said, tamping down on the sigh rising up. "I hope you are well today."

He dipped his head.

"Indeed, I am, Miss Andrews," he beamed. "Even more so for seeing you out today. By the way, who has accompanied you? I do not see your mother about?"

Ever the model citizen, Cashing was obviously wondering about her chaperone.

"Ambrose is at the exchange office for a moment and I dashed out to grab buttons for my mother," she found herself explaining. She wanted to kick herself for it, too. She didn't owe him anything.

"Well, that is hardly safe," he said, chiding her. Her hackles rose and Tillie wanted the conversation to end immediately. "I shall wait with you until you are reunited with you brother."

He finished the sentence and proceeded to fold his meaty arms over his puffy stomach. Unfortunately, Cashing's personality matched his looks. He did not have the sort of profile that graced the pages of her novels and, today especially, his double chin resembled the side of a candle as it melted wax.

She wrinkled her nose at his arrogance. If she needed a companion, it was to chase away men like him.

"That is not necessary," she argued. "I assure you that I am more than capable of finding my way inside and completing my purchases without any oversight."

He shook his head, not hearing any of it.

"It would not be proper," he said, continuing to shake his head so vigorously back and forth she thought he might be having some type of seizure. "What would people think if I let someone soon to be dear to me wander through this particular neighborhood unattended?"

Tillie bristled, her hands clenching.

"Mr. Cashing, I do not know what my father has told you, but —" she began, but he shushed her as he stepped around her, pulled the door open and held it for her expectantly.

Tillie looked around for an exit — any opportunity to escape — but she was well and truly stuck with her unwanted companion now. With a defeated sigh, she rolled her eyes heavenward and stepped through the open door.

To his credit, Cashing gave her a wide enough berth to allow her to move through the store, looking for the items on her imaginary list. She wasn't really looking for thread and buttons, but the story about her mother needing them had gotten her into this situation and would have to get her out.

She managed to take a moment to sneak into the back and have a quick word with the manager. He was quite taken with the design she placed on his desk, and it didn't take more than a couple of minutes for him to confirm that his clients would be more than interested.

She apologized for her lack of professionalism on missing yesterday's meeting, and told him that due to unforeseen circumstances she would have to make today's visit short. She would, however, provide him with a sample of the dress in due time.

When she emerged from the office she saw Cashing looking around for her, but still waiting by the door, as promised. She gave him a quick wave, then presented the unneeded items she had gathered to the woman behind the counter. Tillie smiled and thanked her for wrapping her purchases before turning to leave. Cashing looked impatient as he stood next to the door.

"Finally finished?" he asked, nodding to the package in her hands.

"Quite," she replied with a nod of her head, elated that she had accomplished her task despite all of the obstacles that had threatened her goal.

As they walked out in the crowded street, once again Tillie fought against her natural instinct to run far and fast. Her skin itched being so close to this overburdening man who felt it his right to know what was best for her, despite her protests.

It downright irked her.

"Miss Andrews," Cashing said beside her, clearing his throat. "If I may be so bold, I would like to visit your family this afternoon and speak with your father. You can expect me before tea, I suppose."

Her throat tightened and Tillie felt the panic rising in her chest. Only a fool wouldn't know what Cashing was implying. Only a fool wouldn't know that he was going to ask permission to court her from her father.

But, using the only tactic she had available in the situation, she played the fool.

"Whatever for, Mr. Cashing?" she asked, pasting a smile on her face as she looked up at him.

He gave Tillie a patronizing look, as though he were dealing with a simple child and not a grown woman equal, if not superior, in intellect.

"You shall find out soon enough, my dear," he said, patting her elbow and winking at her. More than any other time in her life, Tillie wished poking someone in the face wasn't frowned upon in public. The man was downright smug.

"Your mother has informed mine that you have been learning more of the domestic arts required to manage a household," he said as they continued walking.

"Some," Tillie said, not wanting to discuss the matter with him of all people. She could practically hear the man's mind whirring away.

"Splendid," he said with a nod. "Capital. All women should possess those skills. It's only a shame you waited so long to finally learn. My sisters knew how to run the household before their eighteenth birthdays."

His sisters had also married men just like him and were probably miserable in their townhomes sewing socks and counting spoons. She knew. She had seen Mrs. Daily and Mrs. Rockforth around town occasionally and neither looked exactly thrilled with life.

"We cannot all be as talented as the former Misses Cashing," she replied dryly instead.

"That is true," Cashing said, completely missing the sarcasm in Tillie's response. "But we do the best with what we have, do we not? You will be fine in due time. You shall see."

Tillie chose to ignore Cashing then, and focus on hopefully spotting Ambrose in the crowd. She was done with this conversation and Cashing clearly wasn't quite taking the hint.

"Where did your brother get off to?" He mumbled, scanning the tops of heads as they milled by. "Quite irresponsible."

She bristled again. It was enough that he took passive aggressive shots at her housekeeping skills, but to repeatedly swipe at her older brother? The one who'd only done what she had told him based on a story she had fabricated? It was nearly more than she could bear.

Tillie was nearly at her breaking point when she spotted Ambrose making his way toward her.

"There is my brother now, Mr. Cashing," she said quickly, stepping away from the bothersome man toward her brother. "I shall take my leave. Thank you for your help."

But, of course, the man wouldn't hear of it.

"Hello, Ambrose," Cashing called out, waving his arms like a damn fool. Heads snapped in their direction from all around at the outburst. "I say, HELLO Ambrose Andrews!"

People were stopping on the sidewalk now, actively staring at the idiot man flailing his arms in an attempt to get Ambrose to see him. Blessedly, because nobody could ignore a spectacle like Heath Cashing permanently, Ambrose finally saw them and waved back, changing course in their direction. As he approached, Cashing stepped forward, likely to offer his opinion on Tillie being allowed out of doors in the first place, but Ambrose stopped him before he could start.

"Cashing," he said curtly with a nod of his head, greeting the other man before turning to his sister. "We need to hurry home. Mamma's sent a message with one of the servants. It appears a gentleman has arrived on the front door with a wish to speak with Father. And you."

Tillie's eyebrows shot up.

"Who is it?"

Ambrose looked bewildered as he spoke.

"Apparently the Duke of Barre is in our sitting room with our father. All have requested your return home post haste."

Tillie smiled victoriously and used the opportunity to dash off toward their waiting carriage with her hand gripping her brother's arm, yanking him forward. She heard the distinct sound of a sputtering Heath Cashing somewhere behind them demanding to know just how in the devil the Duke of Barre knew Miss Andrews and what could he possibly want to speak with her about?

Tillie couldn't wait for him to find out.

6

Tillie knew that this was the plan that she and Alexander had agreed upon. She would send him the note telling him that the deal was on, and then he would arrange everything from there, including their planned engagement. The sooner he came and arranged it, the better, she had thought, as it would mean less time spent mending trousers and dicing vegetables. She knew all this and had been waiting impatiently for him.

So why was she so nervous as she stepped from her carriage and moved toward the door that led into her house? Why did the sight of a much larger, fancier carriage in their stable cause her heart to nearly race out of her chest? Surely, she couldn't be nervous at seeing the Duke of Barre. No, it must just be that she was eager to start everything on the right foot, not making any missteps.

She knew she couldn't be nervous. It wasn't possible. Tillie Andrews was rarely ever nervous. But as her brother turned and held out his hand to help her down, she trembled.

"Are you unwell, Matilda?"

Ambrose had never called her Tillie. He was always so forthright and conscious of decorum that calling his younger sister anything other than her given name was simply unheard of. Still, the sound of her full name on his lips sounded so odd, so very foreign that she began to giggle as soon as her legs were solid underneath her.

He cocked his head as he took her in, and it only made the laughing harder to stop.

"What is the matter with you?"

He wasn't angry with her. No, Ambrose was truly perplexed as the laughing fit grew worse and she clutched his arm as she tried to cover her mouth lest any more embarrassing giggles escape. Even their groom, who had set to unhitching the horses, kept a wary eye on her.

"You need to stop this," Ambrose finally said, placing both his hands on her shoulders. "Whatever fit of madness has suddenly taken over your body, it must stop, Matilda. We have very important people in our home right now and you must pull yourself together. Really. I have never seen you behave like this before."

The words floated past her, but one caught her attention.

"Did you say *people* and not *person*, Ambrose?" The laughter died on her lips.

Relieved that she had at least stopped the laughing, he nodded.

"Quite so."

She waited for him to continue, but he didn't, instead pulling her along to the house, where whoever had accompanied Alexander was waiting as well. She couldn't imagine what her parents were thinking at the moment.

"Who accompanied the Duke of Barre?" She finally had to ask. She couldn't wait for the surprise — she hated surprises.

"The note wasn't specific," he said as he ushered her inside and two maids swarmed her with combs and a new dress. They practically stuffed her into Annie's small chamber that exited just off the kitchen. Annie and Helene now nearly ripped the walking dress off her body to replace it with a simpler, more elegant day dress. It was powder blue with a high bodice and gently puffed capped sleeves over her shoulders.

"What is this about?" She whispered as they tugged and pulled her original clothing off of her. "Why did you push me in here?"

"We're on orders, Miss Andrews," Helene apologized. "Your mother was unaware of what manner of dress you were in when you snuck out of the house with your brother this morning. With a Duke sitting in the salon, she did not want you embarrassing your family with whatever contraption you had dressed in before leaving."

Tillie looked at her with eyebrows raised.

"Her words, Miss, not mine."

Tillie gave a pointed look to the walking dress and then back at the housekeeper, who wilted a little more.

"I know, Miss," she said apologetically. "But your mother gets her ideas and there is nothing we can say to change her mind. According to her, you could have left the house in a linen sack, so we were tasked to attend to you before you made it to the Duke. We were to make you look like a lady."

Tillie sniffed at that comment.

"I always look like a lady, Helene," she frowned, to which Helene actually snorted.

"I've known you since you were nine years old, Matilda Andrews, and one thing you have never been overly concerned with is dressing or acting like a traditional lady," the woman said. "Your mother has a right to be worried, too.

'Tis not every day a Duke and his mother come to call on your family."

For the second time in the space of a quarter hour, Tillie staggered. Did Helene just say that Alexander had brought his mother with him? Was she in on the production, too? She had never met the Dowager Duchess of Barre and had heard very little reports among the local gossips, either. It didn't hurt that Warfield Manor was further away than most aristocratic homes of the *ton*, but there was still very little said or known about the Dowager Duchess.

"This is the best we can do with a comb, a pin, and a bit of pomade," Helene grumbled to Annie. "We are not miracle workers."

Tillie inhaled sharply.

"That will do, Helene," she said, dismissing the women as she walked from the tiny room, her pride smarting just a bit. The walk to their sitting room suddenly felt impossibly long and fraught with danger. What if she misspoke? What if the Dowager Duchess was angry at their plan and had come here to admonish Tillie in front of her family? Her cheeks burned at the thought. Her father would be destroyed and her mother would probably never forgive her.

On she walked, her delicate white kid slippers dragging along the smooth stone of the floor beneath her.

"Nothing to it, Tillie," she sang to herself, a habit of hers since childhood. "Nothing to it but to do it, Tillie."

She hummed the entire walk to the doors that led to the sitting room and even then she stopped and gave pause. It took a gathering of every ounce of strength and courage she had to pull the doors open and walk through. She pasted a large smile on her face to completely hide the fact that her mind was frazzled and her heart was racing loud enough for the neighbors on the next block over to hear.

She looked around the room and immediately found her mother, seated next to her father. Both had a glass of wine in their hands. Odd.

Upon further inspection, Tillie noted the small bubbles fizzing in the golden liquid and deduced it was actually champagne in their glasses. Oh, dear. It was happening.

Her mother looked nervous — her eyes didn't quite reflect the tight smile she was casting. She didn't seem angry, just downright puzzled.

"Matilda, dear, how good of you to join us," her mother said through a strained voice. She was clearly displeased with Tillie, but trying her best not to make it too obvious to their guests, who happened to be seated on the sofa facing them, currently away from Tillie. All she could see of Alexander was the back of his blonde head, seated next to the handsome, low chignon of beautiful silver hair which she presumed belonged to his mother.

She knew she couldn't dawdle. She knew she needed to act to make any of this look somewhat real. And so she did.

One step turned into another as she rounded the side table and joined her parents by her father's side, the smile on her face wide and warm. At least she hoped it was. It was the best she could do with her nerves jangling about in her brain, causing her to breathe shallowly and quickly.

"There you are," Alexander's voice was rich and smooth and so relaxed. Was he feeling none of the nerves she was? "I apologize for not sending word earlier. Mother was so anxious to meet you and your family."

She glanced back at her own mother, daring a peek. Gloria's blue eyes flashed to hers.

"Yes, quite the surprise, Matilda, dear," she said, again a

little too tightly for Tillie's liking. "You might have mentioned your friendship with His Grace before."

"Oh," Tillie said, a little too brightly. "Have I not, though, Mother? I am quite certain I have. We met at Tabitha's wedding. I told you *all* about him, I am sure."

"Yes," her mother said slowly. "Yes, that is right. I must have forgotten. How foolish of me not to remember the man who would appear on our doorstep this morning to propose marriage to my daughter."

Tillie couldn't help her reaction. Her eyes widened and went straight to Alexander, who was trying his best not to smirk.

"Marriage?" Tillie asked, trying to play it off as best she could. "Well, now, that is something."

"That is exactly what I said, dear," her mother half whispered from behind her.

"I know it seems sudden, Mr. and Mrs. Andrews," Alexander was standing now, raising a glass of champagne. "But your daughter has well and truly won my heart and I am a man lost without her. We have spoken of our intentions; however, I wanted to receive your blessing and permission first, along with introducing you to my mother. I understand we have broken all sorts of protocol, but this is a special circumstance, indeed. I simply cannot live without our Matilda here and I am very keen that my mother should come to love her as much as I do."

This was all rather odd. Tillie narrowed her eyes at him. What did his mother have to do with any of this? As though she knew she was in her thoughts, the Dowager Duchess pushed herself to her feet and nodded at Tillie.

"It is a pleasure to meet you, Miss Andrews," she said with an air of stuffiness, as though she wasn't exactly thrilled to be a part of this.

Tillie curtsied. "And you, Your Grace."

"Please. We are to be family, dear. Call me Leticia."

That, however, would never actually happen. Tillie might not be the best guardian of societal decorum, but she knew better than to fall into that trap.

"I am also here for more selfish reasons," Leticia continued, addressing Tillie's mother and father now.

"We have a holiday season full of parties for Warfield Village, home of our own Warfield Manor," she said. "It has been left to me alone these past years to organize the festivities, which are numerous and all important and I fear I am growing too old for it. Alexander travels often to tend to affairs for our estate and I find that I am in desperate need of someone young and vigorous to help see these events through with me. They must go off successfully as our name and reputation are on the line. I would very much appreciate Matilda's assistance. It would also allow me to better get to know my future daughter-in-law."

And there it was. The reason his mother had come after all. Alexander had masterfully plotted a way to ensure that Tillie would have to essentially live at Warfield Manor as a guest of his mother's over the next few weeks while these social gatherings occurred — saving them travel time and hassle and keeping Tillie close by in case the dreaded Eliza made an appearance.

Well played, Alexander, Tillie thought with a smile as she watched the worried look her parents exchanged. Everything about this was unorthodox and simply not done, but the fact that this was such a high-ranking family and they'd shown such serious interest in Tillie had them questioning their reluctance.

Finally, her father spoke.

"You say my daughter will be well looked after? Nothing untoward or unseemly?"

The Dowager Duchess nodded while she spoke.

"My staff and I will ensure that she remains on her very best behavior, along with my son, while visiting Warfield," Leticia said. "You have my word."

It was enough for Gloria, which meant it was enough for Baxter. Within an hour, Tillie was packed for the upcoming holiday season and riding in the grand carriage that had carried Alexander and Dowager Duchess of Barre to her home. Now together, they would all journey toward Warfield Manor, where a holiday season of parties awaited.

7

The ride was long and bumpy. And somewhat awkward.

For all the life-changing discussions and decisions that had just been made in her parent's sitting room, there was little depth to the conversation as they made the day-long journey to Warfield Village.

Tillie sat next to the Dowager Duchess, who spent most of the journey dozing off and on. She smiled at Tillie, but didn't make much effort at conversation, instead seeming somewhat wary of her. Tillie could understand that. She was probably questioning the motives of such a woman who would agree to fake a courtship with her son.

Alexander was his usual charm and smiles, chatting away as he told her about Warfield, the village, his home, and the acquaintances she would soon be meeting at the holiday parties. He told her of the way the house was transformed during the Christmas season, and she smiled at his enthusiasm.

She wanted to ask more about what was expected of her at Warfield, but the addition of his mother to the equation made it awkward, so Tillie bit her tongue and held her silence. Something felt amiss and she wasn't sure what yet. All in good time, she reasoned to herself. Everything, Tillie reminded herself, comes to light in time.

After a few hours she fell asleep herself and was bounced awake by a rather large rut in the road, causing her to smack her head against the side of the carriage she was sleeping on. Alexander reached out and made sure she was all right. Blinking herself back to life, she nodded at him, then looked out the window and took in the scenery, which had changed considerably during her nap.

The rough stone homes were both charming and grand in their own way. They were large and well maintained, but they were also built for country life, to withstand the violent shifts in weather that the north was known for. Forests crept in on the idyllic village as they rolled through the center.

"This is the village of Warfield," Alexander said, jarring her from her thoughts. "The vicarage is just over there and the small array of shops just beyond that."

She followed where he pointed and was instantly charmed by it all. Such a far cry from the noisy, congested streets of London that she was accustomed to.

Almost a half hour later, they arrived at the manor. At least, she assumed the nearly palatial home with the front gates and the immaculate gardens throughout was Warfield Manor.

"Home sweet home," Alexander said, with a grin at her wide-eyed expression. Her family had money, yes, but homes in London were not nearly as grand as the sprawling ancestral estates here in the country. Her father also chose to use most of his wealth to re-invest in his business. The peerage was an entirely different lifestyle.

When they rolled to the front door, a bevy of servants

filed out and waited for instructions as the women and the Duke disembarked from the carriage.

"Welcome home, Your Grace," an older man with salt-and-pepper hair said with a deep bow.

"Pickering," Alexander said with a nod. "This is my fiancée, Miss Andrews. If you could show her to her rooms, that would be wonderful."

Alexander turned to Tillie.

"Pickering is our steward. He will help you with anything you might need."

With that, Alexander left Tillie, a little stunned and disappointed, standing on the front steps with a line of house maids and butlers staring at her from the corners of their eyes.

Recovering quickly, she turned and thanked Pickering, who had motioned for her to follow. They were met in the hallway by a woman who looked to be around Tillie's age, with a shock of gorgeous red curls stuffed beneath a cap, a smattering of freckles, and bright green eyes.

"Miss Andrews, this is Gemma. She has been assigned to you and will see to anything you might need," Pickering gave her a slight bow and was gone, off in the direction that Alexander had strode away, likely with a million questions to ask. Tillie let out a small sigh.

"Chin up, Matilda, dear," the Dowager Duchess' voice came from behind her. "Cannot go about looking defeated your first day. Assume the role and on with it you go."

Leticia was immediately helped by a steward who took her travel bags and followed her through the giant double doors. The line of servants followed the Landon family inside in a swift motion and just like that, Tillie was left standing in an unfamiliar doorway alone with her new maid.

"Are ye unwell, Miss Andrews?"

She blinked and then turned toward the Scottish accent. Gemma's face was kind and she seemed truly concerned.

"I am quite well," Tillie answered,"just a little overwhelmed."

Gemma smiled sympathetically and motioned for Tillie to follow.

"I'll show ye to yer rooms and call up a bath for you," she said kindly. "We'll have ye back to yerself in time for dinner tonight."

To call Warfield Manor a house would be a serious understatement, Tillie mused as she moved through the massive entryway and took in the marbled floors, high ceilings, and candle sconces all over the walls. A castle would be better suited and it fit, as Alexander had mentioned on the ride over that it had been built to defend against roving armies centuries ago.

From what she'd overheard and could see for herself, the place had at least four stories and a large attic. There was a giant underground cellar for wine and food storage that the Dowager Duchess had waxed on about during one of her more-awake spells.

The place was grander than anywhere Tillie had ever stayed and she was suddenly feeling very small. It certainly reiterated the difference between old money and new money, she thought to herself.

Tillie's chamber was as beautiful as the rest of the house. The bed was large and plush, covered in gold blankets and pillows. Curtains were drawn over large windows to keep out the afternoon sun, but some rays peeked in around the edges. The cream walls were covered in paintings of country landscapes, some, Tillie surmised, of the Warfield land surrounding them.

As promised, Gemma had a bath drawn for her. She helped Tillie out of her travel dress and undid the pins that had kept her hair in place. Sinking down in the hot water felt magical and she couldn't help the sigh that escaped. Gemma saw herself out and shut the door behind her, leaving Tillie in blessed silence.

She was relaxing into the water with her eyes closed when she heard a stirring in the far corner.

"I'm just leaving underclothes out for you, Miss," Gemma's voice called softly. "I'll return before dinner to help with yer hair and the gown."

"Thank you," Tillie called without opening her eyes. The warm water was a balm to her sore muscles and she drifted along, enjoying the moment to herself as she undid the day's journey from her body and her mind.

She sighed and dipped her head under the water. Tillie had always loved the feeling of being submerged under the water. She felt free and away from the daily demands down there.

When she slowly resurfaced, she wiped at her eyes, smiling.

"Are you part fish, Miss Andrews?" A different voice said from a corner much closer to her. "I dare say I have never seen a human stay beneath the water so long. I nearly thought I would have to rescue you."

Her eyes flashed open to reveal Alexander slouched against a slightly open doorway she hadn't seen when she first arrived. Letting out a squeak of rage and protest, she dashed lower in the water and covered her bare chest with her arms.

"What do you think you are doing?" she hissed at the Duke. "Are you out of your mind?"

His smirk was back as he shut the door — hidden in the

wall she realized — and crossed the room, sitting down on the floor and leaning back against the bed. They were eye level now, but he was a respectful enough distance away that seeing any parts of her was unlikely. Still, it was awkward for Tillie and she wrapped her arms around herself even tighter.

"Are you comfortable here?" he asked, as though walking in on a woman's bath was quite natural.

She frowned at him, baffled at the question.

"Well," she said, eyeing him suspiciously, "I *was*."

Alexander sucked in a breath and looked toward the ceiling.

"She sent a letter to me earlier this week, Tillie," he said, the conversation quickly changing course, his voice dripping with self pity. The use of her nickname also jarred her. He seemed well and truly upset and this letter from his former love was clearly bothering him.

She chewed her lower lip, wishing more than anything that she could at least get out of the tub and find a robe to wrap herself in. But Alexander seemed to have a lot he needed to say, and didn't seem in a hurry to say it. She remained still and tried not to move.

"There was not much to it," he continued, his hand going through his hair. "But she was warm and friendly and I know she is just trying to reach out to keep a hook in me somehow. If she wanted to reunite with me, she could have easily found me over the past two years. But she knows that we are hosting the upcoming celebrations and she wants to make certain that she is the center of everyone's attentions during them — even mine."

Tillie splashed a little water with her toe.

"If you do not mind me asking," she began, a little quietly as she was still fairly uncomfortable with the entire conversation taking place in the bathing room. "Why did your romance end? Was there some misunderstanding?"

Alexander gave a slow, weak smile. He seemed sad.

"Eliza is beautiful and very smart," he said. "She has been raised to be the flower of everyone's eye and to expect nothing but the best from life. And so, for a brief moment, I must have been the best option around. I was inheriting a title, a small fortune that would sustain me and whatever family I might have for the future as long as I was smart about it, and I like to think that I am reasonably good looking. So I was it for Eliza. She made that clear. And when she had my attention, she had it wholeheartedly. Completely. I was beyond smitten with her."

He paused, taking a slow breath. Despite everything else, her heart hurt for him. And, she had to admit to herself, she was a little jealous of a woman who could so completely capture the love of a man like Alexander.

"But there is always something better on the horizon and he entered into our social circle by happenstance," Alexander continued. "A Duke, like me, but with a bigger fortune, more land. Taller, too, by God. A complete improvement in every sense of the word and suddenly, I was no longer necessary. I had made plans to ask her to marry me. We had talked about it. And then, suddenly, a week or so before I was going to approach her father, she sent me a letter telling me that she no longer felt the same way. That it was time to wish one another the best and move on."

And from the sadness so evident on his face, Eliza must have moved on quickly.

"She made her debut with her new beau shortly after," he gave a mirthless laugh. "There are rumors that she is to be engaged shortly, actually. Which makes her message to me both strange and almost diabolical."

Tillie agreed. If this Eliza woman truly found happiness and moved on with a new duke, why renew a connection with Alexander after breaking his heart so wretchedly? What aim did the woman have? Was she so truly desperate to be the upcoming center of attention, that she needed to be certain that all eyes, including the Duke of Barre's, must be fixed firmly on her?

At the very core of their deal, Tillie had agreed to be more than a fake fiancée. She had agreed to a role that would serve as a sort of protector over Alexander and the story he had just told her made her reconsider everything. This was not just a job to make some freedom money for herself. The Duke had essentially hired her as a bodyguard for his heart, she realized with a laugh. And she was suddenly quite certain that she was going to take her new role very seriously.

If this Miss Masters was hell bent on being the center of attention, Tillie was going to do everything she could to give the little twit a run for her money and to take her down a peg or two. Not only did Alexander's truth open her eyes to how much he was truly hurting despite his carefree and lighthearted demeanor, it galvanized her to not only accept the role, but to truly shine in it for his sake.

"Are you going to respond?" she asked, breaking him from whatever spell he was under. He looked up at her, his eyes a bit clearer than they had been while he recounted his tale.

"Do you think I should?"

She could tell from his voice that Alexander wanted nothing more than to open the lines of communication again with this woman. But that could be a disaster.

"I think you should begin crafting an image that you have quite moved on from her and no longer have time for the previous friendship the two of you once enjoyed. That she no longer has access to that side of you."

"You are quite right," he agreed, nodding along.

"But you have got to be careful not to appear bitter about establishing your boundaries," she said. "So, while I do not think you should respond to her notes, you must be careful not to appear angry or spiteful when you see her."

"Why is that?"

Tillie gave Alexander a knowing smile.

"Because the best revenge in life is to be happy," she said. "Even if you do not quite feel it, the thought of you as happily moved on will hit her where it hurts the most and send a clear message."

Alexander considered her words a moment before standing. In a panic, Tillie sloshed further under water and squeaked in protest.

"Miss Andrews, for a part-fish woman, you are truly brilliant," he said as he turned to go. "Brilliant and wicked."

With that, he winked at her and then was gone, back through the secret door from which he had appeared, leaving Tillie uncertain as to whether she was ever going to be truly alone in her rooms.

8

Alexander had to spend the day attending to business matters for the property, leaving Tillie to wander the halls of Warfield alone for much of the morning. She perused the grand halls full of paintings of the long, distinguished lineage of Landon family members. She made small talk with some of the staff as they moved throughout their own duties, too. Each was kind and helpful, but there was an obvious distance apparent. As if the notion that the Duke of Barre suddenly arriving with a new fiancée was a bit odd.

If only they knew how strange the entire situation really was.

By lunchtime, she was feeling well and truly alone as she ate the afternoon meal by herself in her room, staring out the window at the lush grounds below, wondering what her brothers were doing. Ambrose was likely preparing for his journey, Ethan and Nigel returning from the sea. Christopher was a solicitor and would be at his office, Stephen probably still at home with his family. Thompson was likely doing their father's books, and Max would be in the Andrews' library.

And Mamma? If Tillie knew her mother at all, she knew her mother was probably sitting in her own salon worrying about her only daughter. They had left so abruptly, with little chance to explain anything or leave her parents with a more substantial story while she carried out her mission. But with the circumstances as they were, there had been little to do but kiss her parents goodbye and leave with the Duke and Dowager Duchess of Barre.

Her chest tightened at the thought of how much she was missing her family already. The noise, the closeness, the activity — she'd taken so much for granted.

Gemma returned to take the tray away and paused beside the table where Tillie was staring out the window.

"Pardon me, Miss," she said, tentatively, "but is anything amiss?"

Her question brought Tillie's mind back to the present and she blinked.

"I'm fine, thank you, Gemma," she said, the distraction obvious. "I am just a little lost here."

Gemma glanced cautiously toward the door before putting a hand on the table near Tillie.

"For what it's worth," she said, a little timidly. "There are many of us who are very glad to see ye here."

That caught Tillie's attention and she glanced up.

"Truly?"

Gemma nodded quickly before sparing a second glance at the door — which remained shut.

"I've been here three years now and I remember both the time before Miss Masters and the time after," Gemma said, "and that lass is evil to be sure. She near destroyed the Duke with her games. It was a shame, Miss Andrews, though we were all quite relieved when she brushed him off."

Tillie considered her words. She had heard quite enough of this woman and was ready to meet her.

"Did you see much of Miss Masters?" Tillie couldn't help herself. The curiosity was eating at her.

Gemma nodded.

"Her family stayed here a week or two during the summer festivals in Warfield," she said. "Miserable people, really, for a baron's wife and daughters. Ye'd have thought the Crown Prince himself had arrived instead of her father, the Baron Huntington."

"Is she..." Tillie ventured but stalled. She was almost too embarrassed to ask. "Is she a handsome woman, this Miss Masters?"

Gemma smiled at Tillie.

"Aye, she is a beauty," Gemma said quietly. "But the Duke went and found himself someone far prettier and far kinder than that Miss Masters."

The thought made Tillie smile, even though she was sure it wasn't quite true.

"I believe we are all going to be seeing Miss Masters once again," Tillie said. "I cannot decide whether or not I am looking forward to it, although I should be glad to be rid of the anticipation of the meeting. Alexander – His Grace – sounds shaken when he speaks of her. I hope he does not react too badly when seeing her."

Gemma nodded as in understanding.

"At first, it may be hard," she said. "But with you beside him, he is sure to see what he avoided by not marrying her. Give it time."

Gemma smiled as she turned to leave, pausing at the door.

"There is one other thing, Miss Andrews," she said, turning back to Tillie. "'Tis not my place really, to provide you advice, but as ye 'ave not met her before, I must tell ye that Miss Masters is very good at unnerving people with little comments and slights. My suggestion is to not let her get the upper hand in conversations and to keep her slightly off-balanced."

Tillie thanked the maid and turned back to the window to consider her words. So, this Eliza Masters was a power manipulator in conversations? Tillie considered the battlefield and what her options were once she and her foe came face to face.

ALEXANDER RETURNED to the manor that afternoon with a smile on his face. All was going quite according to plan. Tillie was determined to keep him close in order to stave off Miss Masters.

He looked forward to seeing Tillie again that afternoon, and bounded up the stairs to her chamber, knocking on her door this time. As she opened it, she caught his grinning face and frowned.

"What?" she asked, furrowing her brows, confused at his expression.

"Are you occupied at the moment?" He glanced behind her, as if she might have some object or occupation in plain sight. She shook her head.

"Would you like to join me for tea downstairs? Mother is sleeping, as she usually does in the afternoon, but I have been alone all day and would like your company."

Tillie agreed and followed him downstairs, almost unable to keep up with his long strides.

"Whatever is the hurry?" she asked, a question in her voice. Her legs were much shorter than his and he was practically leaping over two stairs at a time as he made his way to the first floor.

He walked her into the dining room, which the staff had laid out in preparation for the tea service. At the center of the table, Tillie spied a small white box, most obviously the source of Alexander's amusement and enthusiasm.

"Whatever is in the box, Your Grace?" she asked dryly. "A toad?"

The poor man looked utterly confused at her question.

"Why would I put a toad in a box and set it on the table for tea?"

The silence stretched between them a moment.

"Ah. You do not have brothers and sisters," she said, suddenly realizing the truth.

"No, of course not," he said, clearly even more confused.

Tillie smiled.

"I grew up in a household where the moment a male offers you something wrapped in an innocuous-looking box, you question it," she said. "I have received dead bugs, a snake, and three toads in just such a package before."

He looked truly horrified as he absorbed the information.

"It is a miracle you survived, dear Miss Andrews," he said with a grin, shaking his head and composing himself. "No, what I have for you here is much more palatable than a toad, I assure you."

She was interested now and watched as he pulled the twine free and lifted the flap. He tilted the box toward Tillie and it took a serious amount of self control to keep herself from launching toward the gift box and grabbing the delicious-looking treats inside.

She made a move for it and Alexander suddenly had the box in his hand, holding it out of her reach above her head.

"I had thought that I heard you once say how much you like the marzipan from King's. I happened to come across a batch of marzipan I think is better than King's, so I decided to grab us a batch to try," he said, laughing as Tillie jumped and tried to take the box from his hands. "But if you should prefer a toad, I am sure one of the gardeners can fetch one for you."

"Stop it right now, Your Grace," Tillie laughed at his teasing as she attempted to get at her favorite sweet treat.

"Alexander," he corrected her, and he was well and truly laughing now. Tillie finally managed a smile when he lowered the box and offered her a cookie.

She devoured the thing (and another one after that), all with a grin on her face.

He ate his slowly, watching her the entire time.

"What?" she finally asked, noticing he was staring at her.

"I cannot say I have ever met someone who takes as much pleasure from eating a cookie as you do."

If he'd meant to rib her, it didn't work.

"Either you've been eating the wrong food," she responded, "Or you've been associating with the wrong crowds."

9

Two days passed and she and Alexander spent the afternoons together, from tea through to dinner. Many of their conversations revolved around one another, as they learned more about each other's backgrounds, childhoods, and their likes and dislikes. If the world was to know them as an engaged couple, they should have a much greater knowledge of one another. News of their relationship was slowly making its way outside of the immediate village.

Her parents, for certain, had probably been unable to wait much longer than it took Tillie to walk through the front door into the Landon carriage before her mother started telling anybody who would listen that her daughter was going to marry a duke. The word would fly between her mother spreading the news and the fact that in a small village like Warfield, gossip grew wings and traveled fast.

She quickly learned that Alexander had been an athletic child who excelled in anything physical, who hated book learning and who had a mischievous streak.

"It does not sound like much has changed actually," she smirked when he'd told her.

He pretended to look offended and frowned at her.

"And I bet you were an unruly little girl with wild hair and holes in her pinafore," he jabbed back, making her laugh. She couldn't deny it. She'd been a spitfire, as her father liked to say. And whenever left out of the care of their mother, her brothers and father had indulged nearly all of her whims and allowed Tillie to accompany them on whatever outing they had planned for the day. She had hardly realized she was a girl until she turned eight and met Tabitha, who would become her closest of friends.

On the third afternoon, as she sipped from the delicate teacup in front of her, she noticed the tension was back in Alexander's demeanor and she asked him about it.

He was quick to deny it at first, but Tillie wouldn't let him squirm away from her.

"Out with it," she demanded, "what has your knickers in a knot now, Alexander?"

Through their days together, they had become more at ease around one another and she'd dropped the honorifics without really noticing. If he did, Alexander didn't say anything.

"We are having a formal dinner party tomorrow night," he said with a sigh. "We have received confirmation that Eliza and her family will be attending."

Tillie stilled.

"Were they the only ones invited?" From the way he was making it sound, they would be forced to spend the evening entertaining solely Baron Huntington and the Masters family.

Alexander shook his head.

"Three or four other families will dine here, too," he

said. "I am certain it will be as awkward as I have made it to be in my mind."

She could tell he was worried.

Alexander was actually, in fact, a little nervous. This charade had seemed a fine idea, and he had quite enjoyed the past few days alone with Tillie. To have a house of guests was another issue entirely.

"You just need to put on a show for this first dinner," she was saying encouragingly as he mused. "Show her that you have moved on and forgotten her. Just one night and hopefully she will get the message that you are not bait for her hook anymore."

Alexander smiled at her, not the charming, winning smile he bestowed on many women, but a genuine smile of thankfulness. It caused a stirring in the center of her chest, similar to the one that fluttered when they got to laughing together or teasing one another.

"I believe you, Tillie," he said, brightening. "I am very glad you're here."

As much as she didn't think she would be, Tillie was glad also. Her life had gotten a bit predictable and, she'd daresay, boring since Tabitha had married and moved overseas for the next year at least. With her brothers otherwise occupied and moving on with their lives, she had fallen into a lonely sort of routine that didn't include much laughing, or teas, or toads.

"I'm glad I am here as well, Alexander," she said with a smile.

THE SERVANTS WERE IN A TIZZY, running back and forth between the manor's large gathering room that also served as a smaller ballroom for certain occasions (a fact passed along by the Dowager Duchess herself).

Today, the gathering room had been transformed into a splendid dining room with capacity to seat the entirety of their nearly 30-person party at one long table. Tillie had never seen anything so extraordinary put together so quickly. Holly, laurel, rosemary and mistletoe were strung around the room and hanging from the ceiling, a merry fire burning beyond the hearth.

Two hours before the first guests were set to arrive, she found herself downstairs helping Gemma and some of the other maids match the silverware patterns and set out matching sconces for the candles. The Dowager Duchess had asked Tillie to help plan the event, but in truth the servants seemed well practiced at organizing such a dinner. She was content keeping busy setting pinecones and tinsel for a festive centerpiece.

"Ye might want to head upstairs now, Miss," Gemma said as Tillie made to move back to the linen room to get another round of lace coverlets for the sideboards. While it was true that housekeeping was her least favorite pastime — well, next to peeling potatoes — Tillie had helped her mother with enough dinner parties to know how they worked and what was expected. In fact, because her family was so large and invited enough people to fill an auditorium, preparing for large crowds didn't faze her.

"Why?"

She followed Gemma's gaze to the dusty and wrinkled gown she'd been wearing all day and nodded.

"Quite right, Gemma," she said with a nod as she reached back to untie her apron, "quite right."

Her maid followed her upstairs to her room. She shut the door behind them and after Tillie had climbed into the waiting bathtub, Gemma talked as she laid out the clothes Tillie would wear for the party.

"She knows about you."

It was all Gemma said, but Tillie didn't need to ask what she meant by it.

"Are you certain?"

She couldn't deny the rush of adrenaline she felt knowing the game was afoot now that Eliza Masters knew that Alexander had a fiancée.

"Her maids arrived earlier this afternoon to prepare the rooms for her and her mother," Gemma said. "They are to stay overnight. One of them recognized me from the last time they were here and let me have an earful of the drama and carrying on Miss Masters did when she found out the Duke of Barre was engaged."

Tillie couldn't help the smile that curved on her lips.

"So she was...upset?"

Gemma nearly snorted.

"She was near foaming at the mouth from what I heard," the maid laughed and Tillie smiled fully. "It seems Alexander was her second choice should marriage plans fall through with her current Duke."

Good. Let the pampered little princess fret a bit, Tillie thought. Still, her nerves were starting to eat at her and she found herself a bit jumpy. Surely, she had no reason to worry, she reasoned with herself. It was not like her relationship with Alexander, as fun as it was, was real. She wasn't truly being threatened by a bratty aristocrat — she was simply helping Alexander. That was all she was doing, she reasoned.

"Miss Masters is one of those women, ye ken, who men seem to flock to, while women tend to see right through, if ye get what I'm saying," said Gemma.

"Oh, I understand just fine," said Tillie, grateful to have found a friend in Gemma. She realized it wasn't the usual relationship between maid and lady of the house, but she also knew that likely because she wasn't a member of the peerage, Gemma felt she could speak more freely with her.

"And the Dowager Duchess despises her!"

Well that was an interesting piece of news. And maybe it explained why she had not been opposed to this scheme of theirs.

They chose a buttery-yellow dinner dress with a plunging neckline that accentuated Tillie's cleavage and white gloves to match her slippers. Gemma had found the silk blossoms that Tillie had packed, courtesy of an order for a few hats Tabitha had made a year ago, and picked a perfect yellow daisy to add atop her twist. It was striking amongst Tillie's glossy dark locks.

A few moments later, and Gemma was practically gushing.

"Ye look radiant, Miss Andrews," she said with a grin. "Simply perfect. I need to return downstairs to see if they need help, but good luck tonight, Miss. Ye'll do wonderfully."

Tillie thanked her and returned to the vanity for a final look and to settle herself before heading downstairs to start the ruse for real.

She closed her eyes and tried to settle her breathing. Her heart was racing and she couldn't slow it down. Inhale. Exhale. Inhale. Ex—

"I hear a mirror works better when you have your eyes open."

She let out a small shriek and turned quickly to see Alexander in the secret doorway.

"What is back there, anyway?" She asked, peering her

head to get a look. She knew for a fact that Alexander's suites were on the third floor, just above hers.

He glanced behind him into the darkness.

"My father's study — mine now, I suppose," he said with a shrug. "As a child I used to sneak through these hidden passageways to steal sweets from the kitchen and avoid being caught by my nursemaid."

"Clever," Tillie grinned. "Were you here to wish me luck? Is it going to be so awful?"

Alexander shook his head no and instead held out his hand and let a small pendant drop from it.

It was a diamond with an elaborate, jeweled wrapping around it. She squinted toward the jewelry and looked up to Alexander.

"I am actually here to give you this for the evening," he said as he came to stand behind her and drop the necklace in front of her so that it rested in its proper place between her collarbones. As she was admiring it, he moved to close the clasp at the back of her neck and when his fingers brushed her skin, she shivered unconsciously at the touch and their eyes met in the mirror, holding for a moment.

She felt the blush creeping up her face and Alexander cleared his throat.

"The necklace belonged to my grandmother," he said, regaining his composure. "It is for luck."

Tillie smiled, running her finger lightly over the necklace.

"It's beautiful," she whispered, and meant it. She had never seen anything like it.

Their eyes met a second time in the mirror and instead of looking away, she took him in. His dark jacket and cravat were neat and perfectly tied. His hair was in place and his freckles were fading. She actually quite missed them, she thought wistfully as her eyes traveled his face.

"I shall meet you downstairs," he said, breaking the moment, and walked quickly back to the secret door. What had just happened? She couldn't quite name what it was, but something had definitely passed between them. There was something afoot when it came to her own affections. His very nearness was wreaking havoc on her own normally steady composure.

She didn't need to pinch her cheeks now — they were aflame from the encounter with the Duke and surely everyone downstairs would know something was amiss if she arrived looking so flustered.

Tillie waited as long as possible, knowing women like Eliza needed theater and spectacle when they arrived. They needed to command attention, and so Tillie would begin her campaign by taking that bit of power from the woman. Gemma had been instructed to come fetch Tillie only after Eliza and her family arrived for dinner.

Ten minutes into waiting and she was going almost mad. This had been a terrible idea, she reasoned with herself. She shouldn't be late. What if she offended the Dowager Duchess? What if Alexander was embarrassed by her tardiness? She second guessed every bit of her plan and had nearly convinced herself to disregard it completely when there was a knock on her door.

"Miss, it's time."

10

Tillie thought of all of the trouble she and Tabitha had found themselves in over the years. All the roles they'd played to get away with one scheme or another. That's all this was, after all. Just a role she was playing. Tillie Andrews was nothing if not a bit dramatic.

And the curtain was rising.

"It's time," she repeated as she stood and moved toward the door. "It's time. It's just a play acting, Tillie Andrews."

She was beyond nervous now, but her feet keep moving of their own accord, as though they knew she needed to be there for Alexander.

Out her door and to the staircase, her body felt disconnected from her mind as she watched herself take each step toward the gathered group of strangers milling about at the bottom. There seemed to be a sea of faces, but none of them mattered much. She could see Alexander above them all and that was where her feet were taking her.

It seemed everyone stared as she walked by, but she kept her attention on Alexander's profile. It was like a beacon to her, keeping her attention trapped and pulling her close to him.

When she finally approached, she watched him turn his head and saw his eyes light with affection at seeing her. Was the emotion real? It seemed real. And in that moment, Tillie desperately wanted that warmth to be true.

The thought stunned her a moment and she blinked at him as he spoke, missing his words. Shaking her head to clear it, she turned toward the person he was indicating and smiled at the overweight, middle-aged man with a tight dress shirt and a receding hairline. She tried to steal a second glance at his scalp — what was that slicked over his head to cover the missing hair?

"...Lord Huntington," Alexander was saying. Oh. *Oh.* This was really it. Lord Huntington was Lionel Masters, father of Eliza. Lowering herself into the slightest of curtsies to the baron, Tillie murmured a greeting as was polite and returned her attention immediately to her 'fiancé.'

"This is Lady Huntington," Alexander continued, his hand sweeping to a woman with muddy, dishwater-blonde hair that had been finagled into a nest on top of her head. She had harshly kohled eyes that made them look even smaller than they probably were and her wrinkled lips had far too much color on them. She had clearly been beautiful at one point in time but now tried too hard to retain her youth rather than aging gracefully. Her navy blue dress was beautiful, but more suited for a woman Tillie's age.

Tillie rushed through a greeting for the baroness, knowing what was next — meeting the woman she'd been brought here to face in the first place. When she felt the gentle warmth of Alexander's hand on the small of her back, she lifted her gaze to that of Miss Eliza Masters.

Tillie took the moment to truly take in the woman who had apparently so utterly destroyed Alexander's heart.

She was stunning, and Tillie could see why men flocked to her. She had sunny golden hair, which would be a perfect match for Alexander's own. Her flawless porcelain skin had probably never seen a day of amusement outdoors without a bonnet, while her eyes were a warm honey golden brown and her nose was pert and upturned. The cupid's bow of her lip was in a pretty pout she wore as she took in Tillie much the same way.

Eliza had the type of beauty that all women in the upper classes tried to emulate. The men in the crowd glanced her way often, and the way she looked down that upturned nose at Tillie showed exactly what she thought of her. She was the woman all others wanted to be like, yet none really enjoyed the company of — particularly if they knew of her propensity to play games with people's hearts, creating drama amongst the *ton* for her own enjoyment.

"Lovely of you to come," Tillie said with a slight smile. She didn't miss the flash of anger in the woman's eyes at the familiarity Tillie was assuming in welcoming them to Warfield. It was the game she was playing, however, and Eliza was definitely taken aback with her first few plays at power.

"Alexander," Eliza trilled with a smug smile, her eyes never leaving Tillie's. "She is exquisite. You certainly found a pretty one."

Like she was a horse. Or a painting in a gallery.

"She *is* quite exceptional, yes," Alexander said, immediately catching the ice in Eliza's voice. "Tillie is a very special woman, that is certain."

Soon enough, a butler came and called the gathered party to dinner.

Out of some evil twist of fate, Alexander and Tillie were seated directly across from Eliza and her mother. Tillie did not recall the placings set that way earlier in the day, but perhaps she had not paid close enough attention. Eliza's father was at the far end of the table, entangled in a rousing discussion of port and cigars.

At the head of the table, directly on the other side of Alexander, sat the Dowager Duchess, looking bored, annoyed and beautiful all at the same time. If she was as protective and adoring of her son as she seemed to be, it must not have been easy to see the woman who had treated him so poorly seated at her table.

Still, Leticia composed herself expertly, even while blatantly ignoring Eliza throughout the evening. Had Alexander really needed her, Tillie thought, when he had his mother to look out for him?

"It's been far too long since I last saw you, Your Grace," Eliza said between the first two courses. "It has simply been ages. How have you been keeping?"

The Dowager Duchess took a bite and chewed slowly before turning to her and answering.

"Wonderful up until tonight, dear," she said with a bland tone.

Tillie choked back her laughter. She had a hard time knowing if this was Leticia Landon's true personality or if she was punishing Eliza for not only what she'd done, but for showing up at all.

"Tell me, Miss Andrews," Eliza said after the soups were cleared away. "Who is your father? I do not know that I have heard of you before tonight."

Tillie had been expecting this question. Alexander wasn't hiding the fact that her family wasn't from the peerage, but it still pricked at Tillie that Eliza was pulling out this particular weapon from her snotty arsenal.

"My father is Baxter Andrews, Miss Masters," she said as politely as she could.

"He is the shipping magnate who has imported and exported half the goods in London," Leticia said quietly after a bite.

"So you are one of the newly rich, then?" Eliza wouldn't let it go.

"My father is, I suppose," Tillie said with a smile. "He is newly rich because he has earned all of his wealth himself. If we're being perfectly honest, I myself have hardly a penny to my name. But I suppose the same could be said for you."

It had become common knowledge that Eliza's father had no male heir and that his estate would pass to a cousin when he died. By the way her father was shoveling food in his mouth by the handful and washing it down with glasses of port, it may not be long. There was a reason Eliza was out to stay on top and it was more than just winning a game to her. She would have no fortune to speak of once her father died.

It was sad, really, if it weren't happening to such a snake of a woman. Had she truly cared for Alexander in the first place, he would likely have married Eliza and provided more than a comfortable life for her.

The rest of dinner passed in relative peace and after the cakes, the men retreated to the library for cigars and the women moved to the sitting room for sherry.

Tillie faked a headache to avoid further interrogation from the Masters women and retreated to her rooms. After having Gemma help her out of the gown and all its trappings, she allowed the maid to brush out her hair and braid it down her back before leaving.

Tillie wiggled her poor, abused toes and stretched her back. The perfect posture, the too-tight slippers, the snakes at the table — it was all a bit much and Tillie was glad to be at the small table in her room with a few blank pieces of paper in front of her. She hadn't sketched in days and seeing the women tonight in the same fashion from two seasons ago made her long for the hustle and bustle of London tastes.

She worked furiously and filled the pages front and back with loose, free sketches of poses, trying different angles at which fabric could fall in certain cuts. She worked until nearly the entire candle on the table next to her was burned out, and she was drowsy when she finally washed her hands of the pencil smudges in the bowl near her bed.

"I thought you would be sleeping."

She spun at the sound of Alexander's voice, to the corner of her room where he always appeared, and smiled. She'd been thinking about him these past few moments. In fact, Tillie had spent the entire evening thinking about him. Now here he was.

11

"And yet you're here, anyway."

She was smiling when she said it. Tillie wasn't too proud to admit to herself how happy she was to see him.

He walked through the room toward her, his eyes focused on the table where she'd just been working. Instinctively she moved to cover her work, but Alexander was quicker.

"Sketching?"

The question was innocent enough. Alexander knew about her secret occupation, but now she cared what he thought of her work. Did he think it a silly hobby, as did her family?

At her initial hesitation, he put a hand on her shoulder and squeezed.

"Relax, Mademoiselle," he said. "Nicholas told me about how talented you and your friend Tabitha are. He said the two of you are the rave of London matrons and their daughters each season, but are incredibly underpaid and under credited."

She let out a sigh of relief and relaxed, pleased that he respected her profession, though feeling vulnerable at the thought of him seeing her work.

"I prefer that people not know I am behind the designs," she said quietly, her hands wringing. "If my mother knew the full extent of my work, she would probably lock me in my room forever. Or send me to an asylum."

Alexander had the sheets of paper in his hand and was examining them, turning them over and looking at them from different angles.

"These are really good, Tillie," he said, the reverence in his voice sounding genuine. Her cheeks warmed at the praise.

"Thank you," she said, taking the sketches from him. "How did the rest of your evening go? Are you feeling at ease about it all? Was it hard seeing Lord Huntington and his family?"

She really meant Eliza, but she had no interest in saying the woman's name in this moment. This time, this room seemed like it should belong strictly to the two of them.

Alexander considered her question a moment before answering.

"I was not looking forward to it, and I cannot say I fully enjoyed the evening," he finally said. "But it was not nearly as bad as I thought it would be. Surprisingly enough, I felt none of the grief I expected at seeing her again. All in all, it was a bit underwhelming. I believe I have you to thank for that."

That made her very happy to hear.

"I am glad," she said with a smile. "You deserve to be free of that past. It does not serve you well."

With one hand, he returned the sheets of paper to the desk and kept his other hand on her shoulder. The look in his eyes changed from light and unencumbered to a strange look of — regret? — but no, soon all she saw was a burning heat in his eyes as he looked at her. Something inside Alexander shifted as they stood there, looking at one another. What had it been?

"You looked beautiful tonight," he said eventually. She heard his words and she felt the warmth of his hand burning through her thin nightgown and robe. She knew she should have been worried about the inappropriateness of him in her bedchamber. His appearance, however, had become a regular occurrence and now somehow seemed natural.

"You shined brighter than any woman in England, I dare say," he added.

She snorted without meaning to, but the sentiment was ridiculous. She was an average-looking woman with too many opinions and not enough self-control to keep them to herself. She knew she wasn't eclipsing every woman on the continent.

His hand was suddenly gently grasping her chin and urging her to look at him.

"I am not jesting," he said, quiet and serious. "You have managed to captivate me, Matilda Andrews, from the moment I met you. No woman has ever done so in such a way before. What is it that you have done to me?"

She opened her mouth to say that she hadn't done anything — that she'd stuck to their plan to play the doting fiancée. And hadn't Eliza Masters also captivated him in the past?

Alexander quickly kept any words from passing her lips. In a fast, direct movement, he captured her mouth with his own and placed a scorching kiss on her.

She'd never been touched like that by any man before

and her body and mind hardly knew how to react. It felt like every inch of her skin was alight with sensation and a little moan escaped as he slid his tongue past her lips and into her mouth, moving it against hers. It nearly made her toes curl. No, her toes *were* curling. Very much so.

She found herself clinging to his shirt, wanting more from him and not knowing what was next in this little dance he'd initiated. All she knew was that he'd just set her on fire with a simple kiss. Sliding his hand through her hair at the base of her neck, he angled her head just how he wanted it and continued his assault. His mouth was unyielding and invading and the harder he kissed her, the more she needed.

He finally broke the kiss, pulling back away from her. As she opened her eyes, she didn't mistake the stunned look on his face that matched hers. Had the intensity taken him by surprise, too?

"That was..." he began but couldn't seem to finish, "that was not what I had in mind when I stopped in tonight."

Alexander seemed to be trying to explain himself.

"I am not complaining," she said and chewed her lower lip.

He looked at her a moment longer before leaning forward and placing a gentler, more chaste kiss on her bruised lips.

"Neither am I, Matilda," he whispered. "Neither am I."

He took a long step back, though.

"I seem to have forgotten myself as a gentleman," he teased with a wink. "And I would hate to see what your father had in store for me if he knew I was in here stealing kisses from his half-dressed daughter."

She laughed at the thought.

"He would probably assume I had somehow instigated it, actually," she mused.

"I truly did just want to see you before I went to bed," he continued eventually, after a good long look at her. "I wanted to tell you that you made quite the impression on all of our guests. And to tell you that my mother is quite fond of you."

She wasn't certain of that, but she did hope Leticia liked her more than she did Eliza at the very least.

Running her hand across the braid that fell over her shoulder, Tillie's fingertips brushed the pendant that hung around her neck.

"Do not forget your grandmother's necklace," she said and turned around, offering the back of her neck for Alexander to undo the clasp.

She felt his fingertips lightly brush the base of her neck, but nowhere near the clasp of the necklace. Again, the simple intimate caress made her skin feel electric.

"Keep it for a while," he said and she turned back to face him. "It looks perfect on you and hopefully it will bring us good luck. We have quite a few more events to navigate in the coming weeks."

THE NEXT MORNING dawned bright and clear, perfect for the hunting expedition planned. The men gathered their rifles while the women dressed in warm clothing to accompany them to their blinds. The group started out on their walk through the fields, Tillie trying desperately to avoid Eliza Masters. It wasn't long, however, before the woman inserted herself right between Tillie and Alexander.

"Miss Andrews, I meant to remark last night on the beautiful necklace you are wearing," she said with an insincere smile as she took in the jewelry still hanging around

Tillie's neck. "If I recall correctly, it belonged to Alexander's grandmother, did it not?"

Tillie's eyes flew to Alexander's face. Had he previously given the necklace to Eliza to wear?

He cleared his throat, looking at Eliza from the corner of his eye.

"You are correct, Eliza," he said. "You must be recalling my grandmother wearing it before she passed, would that not be so?"

"Yes of course," she said, beaming up at him. "Your grandmother was truly such a lovely woman. I am so grateful to have had the opportunity to have known her so well. I suppose that is the benefit of sharing a common upbringing — you learn so much about one another and your families become wonderfully intertwined."

Tillie rolled her eyes behind Eliza's head, causing Alexander to grin. Eliza smiled prettily back at him, thinking he was responding to her words.

"Miss Andrews," said Eliza, turning towards Tillie, "have you had the opportunity to meet Lord Merryweather?"

"No, I do not believe I have."

"Oh, but you must. He is one of Alex's dearest friends. Come with me."

As Eliza pulled her away, Tillie looked back at Alexander with a pained expression. Her "protection" of him really was not going as planned. Eliza introduced her to Lord Merryweather who was, despite Tillie's misgivings, quite handsome and charming. When they arrived at the hunting site she was laughing at his stories about one of Alexander's childhood exploits when she looked back to see that Eliza had disappeared, as had Alexander.

She excused herself and began to search through the couples for them.

She found Alexander's groom placing his rifles back into the cart. She asked him if he had seen Alexander.

"He has returned to the house," he said. "He was with Miss Masters when she turned her ankle and she had to be accompanied home. He asked me to tell you to continue to enjoy yerself, that he would see you when you returned. My apologies, Miss, that I did not find you sooner."

Tillie nodded her thanks to him and turned away, inwardly seething. She had been bested by the damn woman and she should have seen it coming. She resolved to enjoy the afternoon as Alexander had suggested, but she would prove to Eliza Masters that Matilda Andrews was not a woman to play games with.

ALEXANDER REGRETTED the turn of events that morning. He had never meant to actually pit Eliza against Tillie, nor allow Tillie to feel that she was unwanted. When he had set his plan into motion, he had simply seen Eliza as an excuse to have Tillie stay with him for the holidays.

When Tillie joined them for supper that evening, he didn't miss the glint in her eye as she looked at him, and then at Eliza. He pulled her to the side and tried to explain himself and the situation. Eliza had turned her ankle and had not been able to walk. By the time she had determined she could no longer continue, they were so far behind the group that he had seen no other option than to return with her to the house while he sent his groom ahead to inform Tillie.

Tillie smiled at him sweetly and told him there was nothing to apologize for, but he wasn't fooled. He had come to know her better than that. When she dismissed him by turning to her glass of champagne and the group of ladies she was conversing with, he knew there was trouble brewing.

"Miss Masters, you poor thing," Tillie said as Eliza joined the ladies in the corner of the room. "I was so sorry to hear your ankle did not hold up on the walk to the bluff. It seems, however, to have healed quite well over the course of the day."

"Why yes," Eliza responded, suddenly favoring her left leg. "Alexander was most attentive and his ministrations seemed to have greatly helped."

Tillie held in her snort and resumed her conversation instead.

When they were seated for supper, Tillie found Lord Merryweather on her right, Alexander on her left. Tillie was quite enchanted by the stories of Lord Merryweather. Alexander watched them, surprised at the intensity of the jealousy that coursed through his veins. He had certainly wanted Tillie, that was for certain, but he had not quite realized the depth of his feeling until he saw her laughing at another man.

When Tillie finally turned to him, she told Alexander how much she was enjoying the company of his dear friend, as she placed a hand on the arm of Lord Merryweather.

Alexander had always got on well with his friend, but in this moment he could have clocked Merryweather in the jaw.

In truth, Tillie had been enjoying the stories Lord Merryweather was telling of himself and Alexander. They had been quite mischievous in their youth, and Tillie soaked it up. She didn't miss the set of Alexander's normally smiling jaw, however, and realized with a start he was jealous.

Tillie was not surprised when Alexander showed up in her chamber not long after they retired.

"Ah, my darling fiancé," she said when he appeared, his typically pleasant face drawn together in ire. "How wonderful to have you join me."

"Matilda Andrews," he said as if he was scolding her. "Fake or not, you are here as my fiancée, do you understand?"

"Perfectly," she said. "But if you would like me to keep you from Eliza, I suggest that you do not go gallivanting off alone with her."

"I seem to recall it being your responsibility to keep the woman away from me," he responded with an eyebrow cocked.

"One can only help those who will help themselves," she responded with a lilt in her tone.

"Enough of this," he said as he leaned over her, his face turning serious. "I believe, Miss Andrews, it is time I showed you exactly what it means to be engaged to Alexander Landon."

12

As he leaned down to kiss her, Tillie reached for him just as hungrily. In truth, she had not enjoyed the games played today. She hadn't liked the look on Alexander's face following supper. He was typically so charming and likable, and she had made him act otherwise.

Although she would not argue with the reaction that today's jealousy elicited from him. The passion he kissed her with now went even beyond what he had shown her last night, and she eagerly returned his fervor.

The fact that he cared about another man showing interest in her sent a twinge of excitement through her. She liked to be her own woman, free to do as she chose, yes, but maybe it showed he did care more than he let on.

Her thoughts quickly faded as he pushed her backward and onto the bed. As he continued his assault on her lips, he traced the pad of his thumb along her collarbone, toying with the necklace round her neck. He smelled of spice, of soap, and a masculinity that surrounded her, invading her senses. He overwhelmed her, the taste, smell, and sight of him, and she dug her fingers into his biceps steeled around her head.

This was a side of him he so rarely showed. He typically took everything with light flippancy and charm. Yet tonight he was passion and danger. She reveled in it, soaking it in and drawing all she could from him.

He made love to her mouth as one hand slowly made its way underneath the light fabric of her nightgown, and began caressing her breasts, causing her to gasp.

She reached up and ran her fingers through his hair, drawing him back to her, kissing him as deeply as she could, wanting more of him. As she began to move against him, he responded, one hand slowly making its way up her leg, his fingertips trailing fire as they danced around her calf, her knee, and finally up her thigh.

He waited for her response, ready to stop the moment she told him so, but instead she opened her legs wider and invited him to inch higher. She was no longer thinking, but simply reacting to him and his touch.

His fingers began to caress her very center, and she jerked upward at the shock that went through her system. He instantly stilled, leaning above her and asking if she was all right. "Yes!" she responded, panting. "Do not stop."

He kissed his way back down her stomach and hesitated just at the very core of her. He swiped at her center with his tongue, sending electricity straight through her. She cried out against the intensity of it, but he didn't stop. He spread her open and laved her with his mouth as her hips began moving in sacred rhythm with his mouth.

It didn't take long for Tillie to feel like something inside her was trying to break free. She whimpered and bucked and grabbed the blanket in both hands.

"Just follow it," Alexander insisted. "Let yourself go, Tillie."

With his encouragement, she did and she nearly came off the bed in orbit as the world splintered around her. She'd heard about orgasms of course, from Tabitha, but she'd hardly believed her friend at the time. How could something like that feel so good?

How foolish she'd been for doubting her oldest friend and she swore to herself that she would write Tabitha a note of apology first thing in the morning for not listening to her.

"That," he said with a grin of his own, "is how I treat my fiancée, real or otherwise. Do not forget that, Matilda."

"I do not think I ever could," she said, as he lay beside her, combing his fingers through her long, free locks.

As he rose to leave, she called out his name. "Alexander," she said from her prostrate position on the plush pillows of the bed, "do you not want... something of the same?"

"I am more than satisfied, love," he said. "Sleep well."

As he exited through his secret doorway, she sighed to herself, and rolled over, utterly content.

Over the next few days, Tillie and Alexander attended a dance and a Christmas party in the village, doing the best they could to avoid Eliza Masters and her family, reveling in their newly discovered desire for one another.

At the first dance, Tillie simply observed Eliza attempting to attract Alexander back toward her. She drew the other men to her, her radiant smile and masterful storytelling captivating them. Tillie wasn't particularly impressed, but as long as she had the attention of Alexander, she was quite comfortable with Eliza attracting the rest of them.

At the second party, however, Eliza went beyond what Tillie could forgive.

Tillie was passing by Eliza and her gaggle of suitors when she overheard her words.

"... can you *imagine*, a hat-maker who fancied herself a duchess? Why, I am quite unsure what the woman did to poor Nicholas to force her to marry her, but —"

That was enough. Eliza could embarrass her, say she would about her background, or even her family, as they were used to the barbs of the aristocracy. But to speak about Tabitha in that way? This was something that Tillie would not stand for.

"Eliza," she said, walking up to her with what she hoped was a winning smile on her face. "I could not help but notice your dress. Wherever did you find such a creation?"

"Rochester's, in London," she said with a smug glance. "You should visit the store, Matilda. It is where you can find the latest of what is new and updated in trends."

"How interesting," said Tillie. "I was actually in just last week and saw nothing of the sort."

"You shop at Rochester's?"

"But of course," said Tillie with a pleasant look on her face, although she was far from happy with the woman. "In fact, I purchased a hat there just the other day, designed by Tabitha Fairchild, Duchess of Stowe. While there, I was admiring their newest collection. It is fabulous. I cannot say I saw anything like the dress you are currently wearing."

In truth, Tillie was well aware that Eliza's gown, while quite striking on her, was about two years out of date. Then again, so were most of the dresses women wore around here. Not that Tillie was the type to judge any of them on that basis. In fact, she rather enjoyed the fact that here, unlike in London, a dress could be worn beyond one season in order to extend its life.

However, she was willing to use her knowledge to take Eliza down from the mantel she had placed herself on.

"In fact," Tillie continued, "I believe I owned a dress just like that a couple of seasons ago. It is rather darling, isn't it?"

Eliza's cheeks turned a bright red as she excused herself from the group. Tillie soon had the attention of the young men, as she told delightful stories of London and her brothers and their time at sea. Her laugh, her looks and her countenance drew the crowd, and she was high on the attention and the turn of events.

She was quite content, that is, until she turned and saw Alexander. He was standing against the wall, his arms crossed in front of him and his normally cheerful face in a scowl. When she caught his eye, he turned abruptly and left the room. She excused herself from the men and followed after him, but couldn't locate him anywhere.

She returned to Warfield Manor with the Dowager Duchess and retired for the evening, waiting for him to appear in her bedroom. She knew he was angry, but she was ready to respond to him.

Back in her bedroom reflecting on the evening, she felt rather ashamed, to be honest. It was as if being near Eliza for such a time had poisoned her, drawing her into the depths of pettiness to which Tillie typically refused to stoop.

She wished that Alexander had come to her room so she could apologize and put this to rest. She peeked through the secret door and emerged in the dusty, dark study of the departed Duke. She didn't know, however, where to find the passage that continued to Alexander's chamber.

Instead, she went to bed with a knot of guilt in her stomach, and tossed through the night fitfully, unable to find peaceful rest.

~

THE MORNING DAWNED bright and clear, the winter sun streaming through the evergreens outside of her window. Tillie resolved that today was a new day, and she would find a way to put everything to rights.

The group was to find greenery for the church that morning, and would be meeting at the front steps of Warfield Manor. Tillie didn't see Alexander until she stepped outside. He inclined his head towards her, his expression unreadable. She wanted more than anything to go speak to him, but before she did so, she had something else to do first. It was an action she most dreaded, but knew was necessary.

She made her way down the steps and sought out Eliza, extricating her from the group.

"Miss Masters," Tillie said, turning to face her. "I feel that I must apologize. I should not have spoken to you as I did yesterday. I was upset at the way you were speaking of my friend Tabitha, but that was a poor excuse for lashing out as I did. I do believe that your gown was quite fetching on you, and might I say, you look equally as attractive this morning in that fur and bonnet."

The words said, Tillie turned from Eliza and her startled expression, and rejoined the group, engaging in conversation with the younger daughters of an earl, who was a cousin of the Dowager Duchess. They were spirited young women, and Tillie was enjoying getting to know them during their stay in Warfield.

She longed for Alexander, however. She looked his way,

the soft snow falling on his shock of blonde hair as he laughed with Lord Merryweather. Her heart skipped, and she realized the impossible had happened — she had fallen in love.

She should have known better. It was why she had avoided him following Tabitha's wedding. She knew she might fall for the handsome Duke and his charming ways. It was different now though, she realized. Before it had been his winning smile and his flirtatious compliments. Now it was the man she had come to know so much more intimately.

What to do about it now, she wasn't sure.

They were amidst the evergreens gathering branches when Alexander finally joined her. He took her arm and guided her a short distance from the others.

"Do I want to know what you and Eliza were chatting about on the way here?" he asked.

"I was apologizing," said Tillie, her eyes turned to the tree in front of her. She turned to meet Alexander's blue gaze. "I behaved quite badly yesterday, and I needed to make amends. While she was speaking ill of Tabitha to a good many people, that was no excuse for my behavior."

"I understand the need to defend your friend, but perhaps you enjoyed the attention just as well?"

"It was not the attention from those gentlemen that meant much to me," said Tillie. "The night prior you seemed quite... enamored with me due to your jealousy of Lord Merryweather. I had thought perhaps that provoking your envy might encourage you to me once again, but it seems I overstepped the boundary. For that, I apologize to you as well."

"There is no denying I was jealous," he said. "I would prefer to have your attentions all to myself. However, I also realize why other men are drawn to you. I do not blame you, either, for being yourself. Your natural way captivates people, and as a natural charmer myself," — he gave her a mischievous grin — "I cannot find fault with you for it."

"You are a devil, Alex," she said, "Although I have been very fortunate to be the recipient of your flirtations this past while. I can admit to some jealousy of my own when that turns to another woman, particularly Eliza Masters. To know that she still has enough of a hold on you to cause you to bring me here under the pretense of an engagement says enough."

Alexander cleared his throat, looking away from her before responding. "Until you arrived, Eliza was the fairest of all in this county," he said. "Now that I have brought you here, she no longer holds that title."

"I am not so sure about that, Alex, though it is generous of you to say," she replied.

"It's the truth. Everyone holds you in high esteem, not only for your beauty, but your wit and charm," he said.

"I have never been the type of woman to bring others down in order to build myself up," she said. "She was talking ill of Tabitha and I could no longer hold my peace, but I went about it the wrong way. Forgive me Alex?"

"There is nothing to forgive," he said, then was silent for a moment. He was having an inward debate, and Tillie waited patiently for him to speak.

Alexander turned to her, holding onto her hands but refusing to meet her eyes. "I feel this is all somewhat of my own doing. In fact, I have a bit of a confession to make."

13

Tillie looked at him expectantly as Alexander paused, as if regretting his decision to start down this path of revelation.

"When I asked you to come here, as my fiancée, I told you how grieved I was from Eliza leaving me," he said. "While it is true that she did toy with my affections, and she did leave me for another, Eliza never quite had the hold on my heart I described to you. I was angry when she broke things off, yes, but I was over it soon enough. I also knew her well enough not to fall under her spell again."

"What are you saying?" Tillie looked at him, wide-eyed, and dropped her hands from his. "You lied to me? You brought me here under a ruse, not needing me at all?"

"It depends how you look at it," he responded, a plea entering his eye. "Did I need you? Absolutely. In more ways than I ever thought possible. But did I need you to keep me from falling for Eliza again? No. I know her games, I know the lengths she will go to in order to get what she wants."

"Then why have me here? As your fiancée?"

"Because, Matilda," he said, "I felt something for you, and you rebuked me. I knew that you believed what you were told of my reputation, and I wanted to prove to you that I was not the man you thought I was. I thought perhaps if you joined us here — joined me — you would see me for who I truly am. I knew you had the wrong impression of me from Nicholas and Tabitha's wedding, so in order to change that opinion I had to keep you close. I know this elaborate scheme probably wasn't necessary, but I am not always a patient man when it comes to something I want — and you I want very badly. I knew you would never agree to court me, so I decided to provide you with a backstory that would require your intelligence and your wit."

She looked, at him, stunned. She didn't know whether to be upset at the elaborate lies that he had told her, or flattered that he had wanted her so badly after the short time they had spent together. True, she had developed her own crush on him in that time, and she hadn't seen beyond his reputation, but had protected her heart first.

Now she wasn't sure how to respond. She knew him now, beyond the charming exterior, the wide smile and his flirtatious comments. He was much more than that. She loved him, from the very core of her being. He was kind, he was generous, and he always found the very best in people — even those such as Eliza Masters. He was a good friend to those who needed him, and he knew how to live life to the fullest.

She so desperately now wanted to be part of that life with him. He had admitted he wanted her, but she needed more than that. If she was ever to be married, she wanted an equal love, one in which her husband loved her as much as she loved him. She would settle for that and nothing less.

She also needed trust, to be treated like an equal partner. She felt like somewhat of a fool now. Who else had known about this? His mother to be sure. The servants? His friends and family?

"I — I shall need some time to think on this," she said. "I do not like being lied to, Alexander. Particularly when this scheme of yours called my character into question."

"Tillie, I —"

"Give me time."

With that, she turned, pasted a smile on her face, and left a miserable Duke of Barre staring after her.

On the way back, Eliza stumbled on the snowy path, grabbing onto Alexander's arm for help. She feigned a re-injury of her ankle, but Alexander kindly suggested that Lord Merryweather would be happy to help her back. He was right — the man had no qualms about assisting her back to the manor.

Alexander looked at Tillie, a question in his eyes, but she was lost in thought as she continued down the path. She remained civil to him that evening, and politely requested, out of the hearing of any nearby, that he not come to visit her that night. He nodded in agreement, though she caught a glimpse of pain in his face.

When Tillie entered her bedroom, she so wished she had Tabitha to talk to. Tabitha would know what to do. She was level headed and a wonderful judge of character. If only she wasn't across the channel in Paris.

Gemma came in and helped her begin to undress, removing her skirts, her stomacher, her pockets, and finally her stays.

"I seem to be forever asking ye this, Miss, but is something the matter?" she asked.

"No, Gemma, all is fine," she replied.

"If ye say so," she said. "Ye've got that look in your eye again."

"Whatever do you mean?"

"You're typically the friendly sort, but when you're down, it shows. Ye don't speak and a worried look comes over your face," Gemma said, then paused abruptly. "My apologies, Miss, I should not have said such to you."

Tillie began to tell her there was no issue when she felt moisture on her face. She was not one to cry often, but as one tear fell and then another, she realized she needed to release all of the emotions she had been riding for days now.

Gemma tugged the nightgown over Tillie's head, then sat her down on the bed and asked politely if she felt like speaking about it.

Tillie began to pour the story out to Gemma, including the fact that she thought she had fallen for the Duke. Gemma cocked her head to the side, fairly incredulous, but captivated by the story.

"But Gemma, you must promise not to breathe a word to any of the staff or the villagers," she said.

"Of course not, Miss," Gemma replied. "I donna like to see you so glum. If it helps any, I must say, I believe the Duke to be in love with you as well. A man in love goes to desperate measures to get what he wants, especially a man like the Duke."

"But he lied to me, fabricated this entire story."

"It's not all a lie," said Gemma. "All that's changed is he's a smarter man that he initially let on, not falling for the games of that woman a second time. I'll tell ye, Miss, if I had a duke that looked like him scheming for me, I wouldn't be in my bedroom crying alone."

Tillie laughed at that, wiping her tears and feeling silly

now when Gemma put it so practically. She surprised the girl with a hug and then thanked her, resolved in her decision.

~

TILLIE WAS happy to find Alexander alone at the breakfast table the next morning.

"Good morning," she said with a smile as she sat down across from him.

"Good morning yourself," he said as he put down his tea and looked at her expectantly. "Did you sleep well?"

"I did," she said, then looked up at him and sighed, with a mischievous glint in her eye.

"You know, Alexander, I suppose it should be a comfort to realize that no one is perfect," she said, "not even the Duke of Barre."

He laughed then, the laugh she loved so much, and took her hand and kissed it, relief washing over his face.

"You forgive me then, Tillie?" he asked. At her nod he told her, "Truly, I did not intend for us to be entangled in such a scheme. I only wanted to spend time with you, for us to truly get to know one another."

"I cannot say that I am entirely pleased to have been living in your lie," she said. "But I do understand what your intentions were. You must promise me though, please, Alexander, do not scheme or keep such things from me again. Going forward, we must be founded in truth."

"Agreed," he said with a smile at her as he squeezed her fingertips. "Truth it is."

She smiled at him over their toast, content in the newfound peace they had found in one another.

~

ANOTHER WEEK PASSED as they attended village Christmas parties and dances and Tillie learned to navigate the minefield that was Eliza Masters. Some days she found Eliza to be more aggressive in her game playing and tactics, while other days the woman used her feminine wiles to try to find reasons to elicit sympathy from Alexander. Whether it was a ruined hat or a lost glove, there always seemed to be an emergency that only Alexander could help with.

But, to Tillie's secret surprise and pleasure, Alexander kept her closer. And he visited her at night and tutored her in the art of kissing, though he never went any further, as he had the night he'd shown her the possibilities that awaited her. He told her that he could not so tempt himself a second time.

She did the best she could to keep her mind in the right space, to remember that they were still partners in a business relationship, but the more she spent time with Alexander, the harder that reality became.

She had well and truly fallen for the man, and that could quite possibly spell disaster.

Tillie was in over her head by Christmas Eve. She had been invited (more like implored by the Dowager Duchess) to stay with them for a small gathering in the sitting room to celebrate. By small gathering, she meant the three of them, alone.

An hour after the delicious feast they ate together, the Dowager Duchess made for her bedroom upstairs, leaving Alexander and Tillie alone with their drinks and a roaring fire.

"Does your family usually have a large Christmas?" he

asked the question as they both watched the logs crackle in the fireplace.

Tillie nodded.

"It's my parents' favorite time of year. They never miss a chance to make a fuss for the holidays," she said, "and you?"

He waved his hand around the room they were in.

"My father was never one for celebrating anything, really, and my mother did the best she could to make just the two of us seem like a raucous crowd," he laughed. "But this is mostly what we would do each Christmas. The two of us would sit by the fire and exchange small gifts. We'd attend church on Christmas morning and have a pleasant enough feast with my father. It was quiet. Now, we invite more guests Christmas morning but still keep this night for ourselves."

Tillie marveled at what that must be like.

"I do not think I have ever really known what a quiet house feels like until I came here," she said.

"And I do not know what a house brimming with energy and love would feel like," he replied.

Tillie smiled wistfully.

"It's actually wonderful," she admitted. "Two of my brothers are married, and they come with their wives and children. My family is not exactly orthodox, and the meals are quite the affair. My mother has to join three tables together in order to fit us all, but she is quite determined to ensure we all eat at once, even the little ones. My mother is quite talented on the piano, and after dinner we gather round her and sing. It's uproariously delightful."

"I believe it," Alexander said before trailing off, his attention suddenly on the necklace that hung over her collarbone. He reached a tentative finger out toward it and ran the pad of his thumb over the skin just below it. Tillie sucked in a breath and held it at the contact.

"I find you enchanting, Miss Andrews," Alexander whispered, placing his lips over hers. The kiss began slowly but progressed rather quickly, until it was fast and all consuming, but he stopped suddenly before they could really start.

"Follow me," he said with a mischievous grin as he pulled her to her feet. Tillie put her hand in his and let Alexander lead her to a door toward the far corner of the room. It didn't have a traditional doorknob, and instead, he pushed on the top left corner, causing it to pop open easily. He led her inside a small dark passageway and just before closing the door, he grabbed a candle holder from one of the tables and lit their path.

She realized she was in the secret passageways he used to get through the house and into her rooms undetected.

"Sneaky man," she whispered as they moved up the hidden staircase to the second floor. Occasionally, she could hear voices from adjoining rooms and she would still, but Alexander didn't seem to notice at all and soon they were at the very door he had used to sneak into her room since the first day she arrived.

As though thinking the same thing, when he pushed open the doorway he cast a wistful glance at the now-empty tub in the center of the bathing room.

"I nearly could not walk for a day after seeing you in that tub," he admitted as he closed the door behind her. "Took every bit of self control I had to walk away from you."

He was teasing her, but the look he turned and gave her was no laughing matter.

"I would very much like to kiss you now, Tillie," he whispered. "But I would also like to be a gentleman, and I'm unsure of where this may lead if we start tonight. It's likely best I take my leave."

The thought of him walking out the door at that moment nearly stopped her breath.

"Don't you dare," she whispered as her hands grasped his shirt and she yanked him forward, initiating a toe-curling kiss of her own.

14

"Matilda," Alexander growled against her mouth. "If you do not stop now, you may regret what might result. I could never live with myself if that happened."

Tillie pulled back a bit and glanced up at him, searching his blue eyes for a reason to hang onto any doubts and fears she held. She didn't see a single one.

"Would you regret anything that happened between us, Alexander?"

He groaned and grabbed onto her, as though the sound of his name on her lips had a magical effect.

"Never," he said. "But I am a man and you are a woman and the standards for each of us seem to be slightly stacked in my favor."

She considered a moment and then gave a shrug. She could truly never see herself with anyone but him. If she ended up alone without him, then she still wanted this experience in her life, to have this night with him.

"I have never been surer of anything," she said and pulled hard against him. It was as if the moorings that had held him in check during those long nights of passionate kissing and touching were suddenly loosened and released.

He was no longer tentative and reserved as he reached for her. He moved his hands to her neck and angled her head to the side so that he could place scorching hot kisses down the sensitive side of her throat, causing involuntary shudders and gasps.

"You taste amazing, Tillie," he said, placing punishing little bites along her neck, "and this is only the beginning."

She was in a daze, but a perfectly clear-headed daze at that, so when he stopped once more and took her face in his hands to speak, his eyes boring into hers, she blinked at his words.

"If we do this — if I make love to you, Matilda Andrews — this is it," he said, kissing her lips between words. "The betrothal is not fake. The feelings we are presenting are not fabricated. You are mine. You must be sure that you are ready for that. Because once I make you mine, I am never letting go."

The words stunned her a moment, nearly causing her heart to drop into her feet. Where had this come from? She knew he'd been feeling *something* for her these past weeks, but she had put it down to lust and attraction. From the sounds of his promise, however, the depth of his feelings rivaled her own.

"If we do this, and I decide to *keep* you, Alexander, you will have a hard time escaping *me*," she said. "And I will have just cause to have that twit Eliza Masters tossed in the river if she makes any more overtures toward you."

He laughed and pulled her close.

"Every word out of that saucy mouth makes me want you even more, Matilda," he laughed, pulling her head towards his. "If it would help you understand how ardently I feel about you, I shall toss her and her pompous family out on their ears the moment they return for the New Year festivities. I will not even grant them access to Warfield Manor to appease my power-hungry fiancée."

The words were enough and she found herself tearing at his clothing, despite knowing very little about undressing a grown man. Sure, she knew the pieces of clothing from her siblings and father, but she had little knowledge of the dressing part. This was a whole new world for her.

Blessedly, Alexander had mercy on her and was standing naked before her in mere seconds. She tried not to gape at the sight of him with not a stitch of clothing covering him, but she was doing a poor job. He was simply magnificent — as she knew he would be from her cursory explorations of his form during their tutoring sessions.

The hard planes of his chest led down to a chiseled stomach and a patch of dark hair that led her eyes even further down. She couldn't help herself and she gaped at the sight.

"I am not even certain what I'm supposed to do with *that*," Tillie whispered, suddenly unsure of the entire thing. Alexander laughed and dipped forward for another kiss.

"Do not fret, dear Tillie," he whispered. "I will show you everything. Trust me."

And so she did. To her relief, it turned out Alexander wasn't exactly adept at disrobing her either, and she giggled as she heard him curse under his breath each time a button popped.

"Damn it all, Tillie," he finally said moments before ripping the gown open from the back. "I would curse the designer of this dress if I did not think you created it yourself. I will provide you all the fabric in the world to make ten more of these blasted things if you will just let me at you!"

He had her stripped down to nothing in no time once the gown was off and swooped down and lifted her up, carrying her to her large bed and depositing her in the center of it.

Tillie suddenly felt shy of her nakedness as she lay on her back in the center of the bed, but when she tried to squirm to cover up, Alexander stilled her with his warm hands on her legs.

"You are beautiful, love," he whispered as he placed a burning kiss on the inside of her knee. "Let me look at you. Let me savor this."

And Alexander savored. His mouth kissed up and down her legs, across her stomach, and all over her collarbone. His lips made special stops at her rosy nipples where he sucked and nibbled the sensitive buds and nearly had her going out of her mind with lust, grinding her hips against his as the pressure began to build in her body.

He smiled wickedly at her and resumed his ministrations, slowly circling her. He plunged a finger into her damp folds, and she moaned loudly. He covered her mouth with his, drinking in the sounds she made.

She felt heat building throughout her body, and suddenly the explosion began in her middle and seemed to travel out to every part of her, from her fingers to her toes.

Quivering from the aftershocks, she nearly giggled in excitement as Alexander moved up her body to press his mouth to hers, plundering her with a kiss that brought her back to her senses, ready for another go. With his mouth and his hands, he had her slick in no time and he braced his elbow next to her head while his hand guided the tip of himself to her entrance.

"It will hurt, but only for a moment," he said. "I'll go slowly for you, love."

Tillie nodded at him.

"You are mine now," he said as he inched forward, breaching her barrier. She gasped at the sting as it gave way. "You are mine forever now, Matilda Andrews."

In no time, he'd slid his impressive length all the way to the hilt until he was seated fully inside her. The feeling of being so full of Alexander, of being stretched in such an intimate way, was mind blowing and Tillie couldn't help but wrap her legs around his waist and try to take in more of him — to take every last piece of what he had to offer.

Sure, she belonged to him now, but Alexander equally belonged to her.

"So tight, love," Alexander rasped, as though he was fighting the urge to move. "You feel like heaven."

They remained still while she adjusted to the sensation, but it wasn't long before she was arching her hips up toward him and trying to use her legs to coerce him to move. Thankfully, Alexander took the hint and slowly pulled himself out before smoothly pushing back in.

She moaned loudly.

The pain was completely gone and replaced with pure pleasure. It was as if Alexander's perfect body had been made for hers, they fit together so well.

He was obviously holding back and she wanted all of him, wanted everything he had to give her, so Tillie used her legs to pull him harder into her, the intent clear.

Like a man possessed, Alexander powered into her with deep, glorious strokes. She moved against his power and loved the feeling of her breasts bouncing against his thrusts, which were hard and fast.

His breathing was ragged now and she wondered if he was getting close to his own orgasm when he reached between their bodies and found the magical spot on her own sex that he'd toyed with earlier. With a few deft flicks of his thumb, Tillie was catapulted into a second, more powerful orgasm that had her shouting Alexander's name into his shoulder to muffle the sound.

Two, three, four more powerful strokes after that and he roared his own orgasm into the pillow beside her. His body twitched as he poured his seed into her and she found the idea of him claiming her so thoroughly to be incredibly arousing.

He groaned into her pillow and pushed himself on his elbows before raining kisses down on her face.

"I love you, Matilda Andrews," he said, his voice heavy and thick with emotion. "I didn't plan to, but I do."

She couldn't speak the words yet, but the tear rolling down her cheek spoke for her.

15

When she woke the morning after their love making, Tillie panicked. They had fallen asleep together in her bed and she heard the sounds of servants moving through the house. She shot up in bed, remembering the night they'd had that had gone on into the wee hours. It was dark in her room; had he left her?

A hand shot out from beneath the covers and Alexander pulled her back down into his arms.

"It's almost as if I can hear all those worries in your head," he grumbled, his voice gravelly with sleep. "Calm down, love. I shall be back in my own room before your maid gets here, though I daresay I am not really worried about her opinions of what we do."

Her cheeks reddened again when she recalled what they had done, and how badly she wanted to do them again. There was no time for that, however, as they had to ready themselves to celebrate Christmas. Tillie was much more concerned than Alexander on what the servants thought of her, and she pushed him out of her room before Gemma arrived to help her dress.

The Christmas Day service was as special as Tillie had hoped it would be. The chapel was filled with villagers of every station, coming together to celebrate the special day.

They returned to Warfield Manor along with many guests for a Christmas Feast, Christmastide truly having begun. While the Landons enjoyed the first night of the 12-day celebration, Christmas Eve, as a small family affair, they began to celebrate the season in earnest the following day.

The Yule Log lit the evening before continued to burn in the fireplace, and Tillie gazed at it wistfully, as its fire began the same night as the love which began burning so much brighter between her and Alexander.

As they were already known to be engaged, the little shows of real affection between them did not necessarily set tongues to wagging. If anything, the people around them seemed wistful of the way they doted on one another.

The Dowager Duchess was the only one who seemed slightly surprised, but she did well to hide her smile when she saw how the two of them were getting on with one another.

A FEW DAYS AFTER CHRISTMAS, Eliza and her family, along with assorted other guests from surrounding villages and from as far as London, began gathering at Warfield Manor for the annual New Year's Dance and celebration.

As far as the former contract had been concerned, it was nearing an end as the final event would be the Twelfth Night. The celebration would be the last in which they were to perform as a couple to end out the holiday season that Alexander had gone to such lengths to have Tillie attend.

But so much had changed in both of them now.

Tillie hardly paid attention through the first meal in the house with all of their assembled guests, she was so absolutely giddy with anticipation and joy. Her feelings for Alexander, and apparently the ones he felt for her, seemed to take them both by surprise, and all of the late-night sneaking had made the entire thing so much more fun.

Tillie could scarcely believe it, but she was at a point in her life that marriage actually sounded like a wonderful, freeing thing instead of the opposite.

That evening, as she prepared with Gemma for the dance, a knock sounded at her bedroom door. When Gemma went to open it, one of Alexander's valets was standing there with a box, which Gemma took.

"I don't need to ask what this is, do I?" the maid asked the valet, who simply smirked.

There was a small piece of paper attached to the box and Gemma handed it to Tillie without looking at it. Pulling it open, Tillie read the words written in Alexander's graceful handwriting.

"I plan on seeing you wearing this later. This, and only this."

She quickly tucked the note into her desk and hid it among her sketching supplies before returning to the box while Gemma pulled all of her accessories out for the night.

"Please do not be a toad. Please do not be a toad." She whispered to the small square box as Gemma looked at her as if she had gone mad.

When she pulled the lid off, a beautiful gold cuff bracelet dotted with diamonds sparkled on a silk pillow. It was breathtaking.

"Oh, Miss," Gemma cooed behind her. "What a lovely gift."

Tillie couldn't help but blush at the memory of his note, too.

Gemma and Tillie had worked diligently on the gown she would wear for this dance and when it was finally on, she smiled at their work. It was a simple cut with a high bodice that hung off the shoulders, but what she and her maid had managed to do was attach a layer over the skirt that had been sewn with small, shimmering jewels to create the effect of stars. The gown itself was a deep navy blue and instead of flowers in her hair, Gemma dotted the softly curled tendrils of her hair with more of the same shining costume jewels Tillie had brought from London.

"You glow, Miss," Gemma said with a sharp intake of breath. "You are simply glowing."

She took a turn in the mirror and beamed at the dress she'd fashioned. It was truly one of her best and she was so glad she had decided to keep it for herself.

Fully dressed, Tillie let Gemma return to her duties downstairs and waited for a valet to come collect her. When the knock came, she opened the door to find Alexander there instead of a servant.

"But I thought—" she began, but was silenced with a kiss as Alexander pushed her back into her room and shut the door behind him.

When he broke the kiss, he held her at arm's length and took a long look at her from head to toe and she blushed under his scrutiny.

"Beautiful does not do you justice, Tillie," he said in a quiet, reverent voice. "For the rest of my life, I shall never forget the way you look tonight."

Emotions roiled through Tillie. If she thought she'd had feelings for Alexander a week ago, two weeks ago, it was nothing compared to what she felt now or likely would feel in the coming days.

"I am quite proud to have you as my fiancée," he said, offering his arm. "Fake or otherwise."

"I love you, Alexander Landon, Duke of This-and-That and All-Other-Sorts-of-Things," she said as she couldn't resist a little bit of ribbing.

"Barre," he said with a laugh. "Just Barre. You best get used to the title, my future duchess."

The Dowager Duchess watched them that evening with a smile on her face. Her son had found a woman worthy of him, and she was happy for it. True, Tillie had no title to her name, but she had the manners of a peer, and the ability to do what other ladies of the *ton* had not — capture Alexander's heart.

The dance began and Tillie, for once, enjoyed herself, as there was no Heath Cashing to hide from and no disapproving parents or siblings to tell her that she wasn't being social enough or that she was being too overly social. There was only Alexander and he was everything she had never known she had wanted or needed.

So, naturally, of course, it was bound to fall apart because Matilda Andrews was never one to fully believe in fairy tales and happily-ever-afters that were unearned.

A couple of hours into the celebration, a valet approached Alexander as he and Tillie were standing in conversation with some of the villagers from Warfield. The man whispered into Alexander's ear and she watched as the Duke's eyebrows shot skyward. Whatever he had just been told had taken him completely by surprise.

He turned to Tillie and pulled her away from their conversation momentarily.

"A friend from school has just arrived at the back door in bad shape," he said, rather cryptically. "He is a noble and when they arrive bloodied and beaten on your doorstep, it's never good. Try to keep the party from noticing my absence, love?"

She was worried but gave him a quick nod. She would do what she could, but now she was concerned. Who was the man? Why was he injured? And would Alexander tell her who he was?

In a flash, the Duke was gone and she was left entertaining the guests. As was polite, Tillie danced with a few of the partygoers and tried to help the Dowager Duchess with hosting duties, all the while searching the corners of the hall for signs of Alexander.

But there were none.

He had completely disappeared from the party.

Tillie nervously ran her hand over the bracelet he'd given her earlier and fretted. It had been more than an hour now. Was something wrong?

Never one to wait around for something to happen, Tillie made her excuses and left the ballroom, finding her way through a series of servant hallways, not really knowing where she was headed or what she was doing, but feeling a pull to find Alexander and make certain he wasn't in trouble.

It took her a good ten minutes of wandering through the passageways and hiding in the shadows when a maid came rushing by with a tray of empty glasses before she finally found what she was looking for. A valet came running through the hall with a stack of linen towels.

Staying far behind, she followed the young man through a line of twists and turns and held back as he slipped inside a door without completely shutting it behind him. Tillie crept forward and quietly peered into the dimly lit room.

There were servants milling around in a hive of activity that Tillie could hardly make sense of. On the floor against a far wall was a pile of bloody bandages. She followed the path toward its source and saw a man, not much older than herself, lying unconscious atop a small couch, his massive arms and legs draped over the sides. Part of his shirt had been ripped away and she saw a large, bloody wound that the servants were trying to treat the best they could.

Another man stood near the back, looking equally disheveled but not nearly as bloody, pacing in front of the window.

"Where is the doctor?" he inquired of Alexander's servants. "And where did Barre disappear to? We need him!"

"My Lord," one of the valets spoke up. "The Duke's fiancée called him and he went to assist her momentarily. He should return at any moment."

Fiancée? She hadn't sent a notice for Alexander. It took her not longer than a moment to discern who else could possibly have sent for him. She realized she hadn't seen Eliza in the past hour at the dance.

Cursing, she set off in a tear to find her fiancé.

16

Figuring Eliza had tricked him somehow, Tillie knew she wasn't going to find them in the servant's hallway, so she exited into the sitting room. Setting her skirts to right and smoothing her hair, she took a brief moment to compose herself before beginning her search anew. She not only had to find Alexander, but he must explain what was occurring with the injured man, and why would Eliza not let him be?

She thought about which rooms Eliza would be familiar with and also would make sense for Tillie to call him to. The options were limited.

Guessing Eliza would have chosen the library to lure Alexander, Tillie raced over the carpeted hallways, away from the dancing and the music. Her heart thumped in her chest as she worried over what might await her, fearing her life and happiness depended on it. Because, unfortunately, it did.

The door to the library was just ahead and for a brief second, Tillie considered what she was doing. What if she saw something on the other side that shattered her heart?

Alexander had said he'd loved her, so she should have no fears. Yet, she told herself, he had put his love into words in the heat of their lovemaking. Did he truly mean it?

She questioned herself about whether she should open the door. What if it she saw something that could never be undone? Was she willing to risk losing this sense of peace and happiness she'd managed to find with Alexander in order to know the truth?

Yes, damn it all. Tillie wasn't one to live in half-truths, shadows, or deceit and she damn sure wasn't going to start now, heartbreak or no.

Shoving the door open, she braced for impact and yet was nearly staggered by the image in front of her.

They were sitting on the settee, Eliza's skirts settling to the floor around them. Eliza was sobbing, naturally, because that was her currency. It was how she reined in the males in her life. She was clutching at the lapels of Alexander's jacket as he held her in an embrace.

Tillie wanted to scream. She wanted to be sick. She wanted to rage. Instead, she spoke quietly and slowly.

"Oh," she began, her voice emotionless and deadly. "I see you received the summons from your betrothed, Alexander. How wonderful."

His eyes snapped to hers and he all but shoved Eliza away from him.

"No, please, do not let me interrupt," Tillie said coldly, holding up a hand. "Forget you saw me. Forget this – *any* of this – ever happened."

She turned and dashed for the door and had gotten a few feet down the hallway when Alexander's long strides caught up with her.

"Tillie, please," he pleaded as he grabbed her wrist. "It is not what you think at all. I thought it was you who had summoned me."

She narrowed her eyes at him.

"So you get to the library, see that it's *her* and pull her into your arms? How reasonable and noble of you, Your Grace," she seethed, her heart shattering. His face looked stricken at the formality back in her tone.

"She jumped at me in a flurry of tears, Tillie," he cried out, frustrated.

She just shook her head, unwilling to hear any more.

"You have a man bleeding to death in one of your hidden rooms," she continued and if it was possible for him to look even more surprised, he did. "A friend of yours? Another secret meeting you had planned? Care to tell me what is going on tonight before I walk out that front door and never return?"

Alexander's mouth opened and closed.

"Do not overreact, Tillie. You cannot leave me," he said, his voice quiet but resolute. "I will not allow it."

She smirked.

"You cannot tell me where I can and cannot go, no matter who you are to me. However, if you do not want me to leave, tell me what is going on right now," she insisted. "Tell me who the man with the bullet wound is. Tell me why Eliza Masters is trying to throw herself at you and why, despite your protestations you would never go back to her, you were holding her in your arms. Tell me that you trust me enough to want me to stay by your side."

There was no mistaking the emotion and internal war in his eyes. He was struggling with something, but he wouldn't let Tillie in.

"I cannot, Tillie," he rasped. "Please. Please, understand. I will tell you when I can."

She studied his face.

"Do not shut me out, Alexander," she said, the anger leaving her voice and the raw emotion settling in. "If you do, there will be no turning back."

He reached out and put both hands on her shoulders. Just as he moved to speak again, a footman ran through a doorway a few feet behind them.

"My apologies, Your Grace, but you are needed immediately," the man said. "Please, hurry."

Alexander closed his eyes and cursed.

"Please, Tillie, do not be rash," he whispered as he pressed a hot kiss to her lips before she could pull away. "Please trust me. Don't you dare try to leave right now."

Without another word, he turned and ran toward the footman, leaving Tillie standing alone in the hallway, unsure of what had just happened and where she currently stood.

So Tillie did what she always did when someone gave her an order — the opposite. She left.

17

She had not arrived with much and she left with even less.

Tillie also didn't try to hide the fact that she was leaving and marched out the front doors to the carriage house, demanding a ride to London from one of the grooms.

"Miss Andrews," the poor man stammered, "'tis the middle of the night! Perhaps if we wait until the morning and when His Grace is available, we can secure you a ride. It is not safe for you to leave now!"

With heavy bag in one hand and a broken heart in her chest, she set her mouth in a grim line, and spoke evenly and calmly, despite the storm roiling in her.

"I appreciate your concern, but if you do not give me a ride to London this instant, I will start walking down that road and not stop until I reach my destination or get set upon by wild animals."

In the space of a few seconds, when it seemed the man wouldn't budge, Tillie decided to make good on her threat and turned to begin walking away from Warfield Manor and its village. The place had utterly broken her heart and she was ready to be done with it.

She got further than she had expected to, but was relieved that the groom finally caved.

"Please! Please, Miss Andrews!" he said, chasing after her. "I'll get you a carriage ready. Please don't walk away in the dark!"

The journey back was long and bumpy in the dark as the poor driver navigated the rough roads with very little light, but in the back seat, Tillie wasn't paying much attention. Her mind was revisiting the scene she'd stumbled upon over and over again.

It wasn't so much that she believed what she saw. She was smart enough to know Eliza's schemes and was fairly certain that Alexander did, too. No, what was the most troubling to her was the fact that there was still a chord for Eliza to yank between them that would get any sort of reaction from Alexander. He had told her that he wasn't truly grieved by their broken relationship. Tillie thought that connection between Alexander and Eliza was finished. Now, seeing how it remained, she questioned if what she and Alexander had was as real as she had believed.

And the injured man in the secret room. Who was Alexander Landon that bloody nobles arrived on his doorstep in the middle of a party on New Year's Eve? And who were they that she could not be trusted to know what was going on?

To Tillie, as she rode the miserable journey back to her parents' house, the fact that there was so much of Alexander's life that he was unwilling to open up to her about was a cut even deeper than seeing Eliza wrapped in his embrace for comfort.

The tears began as the carriage traveled overnight and

more than once, she found herself wishing beyond reason that she'd hear a thunder of hooves outside the small window to find a distraught Alexander chasing her down.

But, alas, the only noises she heard were owls in the distance and the constant of the hooves of the carriage's own horses.

No, by the time the carriage pulled up in front of her father's home, Tillie was quite certain that the game was over and her time to return to her own life, sad as it was, had arrived. She had been played, another conquest of Alexander Landon. What a silly twit she was.

Worse, she still loved him. Sick to her stomach and the heart in her chest aching, she disembarked from the carriage just as the sun was peeking its way through the sky in the distance.

At the front door, her father took the small bag the driver handed him and her mother opened her arms for an embrace which Tillie ran into, tears starting afresh.

SHE CONFESSED the entire thing in her family's sitting room – well, nearly the entire thing. She left out the late-night liaisons. With her head in mother's lap, she poured out her heart to her parents and prayed they would find it within themselves to eventually forgive her. She was ashamed of herself and heartbroken all at the same time.

"I was such a fool," she sobbed as her mother stroked her hair. "I thought I was so very clever — that I could have my own way and have a life that I wanted and made for myself."

Her tears wouldn't stop and it seemed to be more than her father could bear. He pushed himself to his feet and paced back and forth around the room, nearly wearing a path in the carpeting.

"You say you love him? And that he loves you?"

She had believed those statements to be true. She really had.

"I cannot be sure now," she said. "I do love him, yes. As for how he feels — I am not sure. He was keeping so much from me."

Her father scrubbed a hand over his face and sighed.

"Matilda Olive Andrews," he said. She braced at the sound of her entire name, despite the gentle tone. "I am sorry."

She blinked. Her father was apologizing. For what? She looked to him as her mother stroked her back.

"I am sorry I did not trust you to make decisions for yourself, so much so that you would help concoct a plan as creative and deceptive as the one that took you to Warfield," he said. "I should be furious at you and I partly am, especially since you were willing to walk the roads in the middle of the night to get back here, but mostly I am sorry that I didn't trust you with your own life. Take your time, girl, in the next few days, and really think about what you want. I will not force you to marry and if you choose to get old and take care of your mother and me for the rest of your days, so be it. It will be your own choice."

They were the words she'd always wanted to hear, but now they seemed to come too late, when what Tillie really wanted was to be the wife of a man who seemed so unreachable now.

"Take your time and heal your heart," her father continued. "And if that Duke is worth any bit of his noble blood, he shall be on my doorstep in the next few hours begging your forgiveness. No notes. No servants. You will accept nothing less than the man himself, and only if you choose to do so, do you understand?"

She nodded through her tears, though not believing she would hear from Alexander anytime soon. He was wrapped up in his own life — one that didn't seem to have space for her when it really mattered.

ALEXANDER HAD BEEN DISTRAUGHT when he was told Tillie had left in the middle of the night. He was angry at her for not trusting him, and for leaving without regard for her own safety. He was angry with himself for letting her go and not giving her the total truth. And he was certainly angry with Eliza for her games, although he realized he likely should have thrown her out ages ago, and probably should never have allowed her family to come in the first place.

He was tempted to chase after Tillie that night, but he knew she was with a trustworthy groom, and he had issues of his own at the manor to look after. Issues that included a dying man and a tormented friend. Leaving was not an option, and he knew Tillie, while angry, wasn't in any immediate danger.

He did, however, send a flurry of notes after her, asking for her forgiveness, her return, and her understanding. He heard nothing back. Not a word. He could understand her reaction to the scene she had walked in on, but he also felt she owed him the chance to explain himself. He wished she could have trusted him to do as he saw fit. Although, he supposed, she likely had hoped just as much that he would trust her to tell her the truth of the matter.

He sighed. Part of the reason he had let her go, and stay away, was also that he wanted to protect her. There was much happening that he was unsure of, and he didn't want to risk Tillie's life or well-being. The safest place she could be was away from him in London.

The moment he had everything sorted out at Warfield Manor, he was in his carriage, urging his groom to make for London as fast as he could push the horses. He hated the days that had gone by with so much unresolved between them, and only the extenuating circumstances could have kept him from Tillie. He ached to see her again, to hold her again, and to make sure he knew how she truly felt about him. He couldn't stand to have another day go by without her by his side.

He wanted answers regarding her silence, and he would provide her with the explanation she sought. First, he had to convince her to listen to him. He began to formulate a plan in his mind.

ALEXANDER LANDON, Duke of Barre, had never been quite as nervous as when he knocked on the door of the Andrews home in London. It was an impressive house, particularly for a family outside of the aristocracy. He had great respect for Baxter Andrews, who had made his own way in the world, from a carpenter's son to a shrewd businessman.

Alexander knew it would take more than calling upon Tillie to have her speak to him. He just wondered how many of her brothers he would have to go through to get to her.

The butler brought him into the house, and left him in the sitting room while he found Baxter. Alexander was tapping his foot when the man walked into the room, flanked by six of his sons. Alexander stood abruptly at the seven men in front of him. How fortunate it was the holiday season, he thought sarcastically. They all seemed to be at home.

"Duke of Barre," Baxter said, with emphasis on the "Duke." "You've finally arrived. Please, sit. You may not be familiar with all of my sons. Maxfield, Ethan, Nigel, Christopher, Stephen, and Thompson. Ambrose is currently — otherwise occupied."

"How wonderful to make your acquaintance, sirs," said Alexander, with a slight bow to the men, some who sat next to their father on the chesterfield, the others lounging about the room on various pieces of furniture, or standing against the wall. "Tillie — Matilda — has told me so much about you all." Including how protective of her they were, he thought, although he didn't voice that concern out loud.

"I have heard much of you as well, Duke," Nigel replied. "None of it of late has been much good, I'm afraid."

Alexander nodded his understanding to him. "I apologize," he said. "Tillie and I did not part on the best of terms, but I hope to change this. May I speak with her?"

"Matilda is not in at the moment," said Baxter. "What do you wish to say to her that has taken you four days to determine?"

"To be fair sir, I tried to send messages —"

"I am aware."

"There were circumstances at Warfield that I did not want Tillie exposed to," he said cryptically. Seeing Baxter required more of an explanation, Alexander told him what he could of the night Tillie had left, of what had transpired regarding the injured man and his own friend.

"You say you allowed her to leave your home for her own safety," said Ethan. "That leaves us with serious misgivings about entrusting her in your care in the future."

"The situation is rectified, Mr. Andrews," Alexander

said. "I would never put Tillie in harm's way. And, to be fair, Tillie will always care for herself. I would simply aid in that endeavor."

"What do you want now?" asked another brother. Alexander thought it was Christopher, but he couldn't be sure.

"What is most important, Mr. Andrews," he said, addressing Baxter, "Is that I love your daughter, and I would very much like to make her my wife. Do I have your permission?"

Baxter studied him, taking measure of him. He seemed to be satisfied with what he found.

"You have my permission," he said with a nod. "But most importantly, you must acquire hers."

Alexander nodded. "For that, I may need some assistance."

18

Four days.

Not a single word in four bloody days, Tillie groused as she crumpled another sheet of paper in the freezing cold storeroom of her father's office building. She used the abandoned room as a makeshift studio when her own home was too loud and chaotic and she'd sought out a little peace a few days after arriving back from Warfield.

Mostly, she just wanted to be out of the house because it was a constant reminder that Alexander hadn't come for her. That he wasn't coming for her. All of her brothers were also home, and they all tiptoed around her as if she were a porcelain doll. She was quite exasperated with it all.

She'd stabbed herself with stick pins more times than she cared to count and the cold was making her extremities numb.

Tillie knew she needed to return home but she couldn't bring herself to do it, despite the danger of catching her death of a cold from the drafty, freezing conditions she worked in.

Death from a cold would be much more acceptable to her now than death from a broken heart.

"Pitiful," she cursed at her bleeding fingers as she slid into the chair behind her and laid her head on the desk, biting her lip to keep from crying. Again. She was a lost cause at this point and she was certain she was doomed to spend the rest of her life alternating between sewing her father's socks and collapsing into a soggy emotional puddle at a moment's notice.

Drawing in a breath, she pushed herself to her feet and began to tidy the desk. It didn't matter, nobody used the space but her, but she hated to see all of her supplies in disarray, even if they were a good metaphor for her emotions and sanity at this point.

Ambrose appeared in the doorway and cleared his throat.

She swiped at her eyes and looked up.

"Yes?"

The worry on his face was evident. All of her brothers were worried about her, even Max, who set his book down whenever she walked into the room to wait for the next emotional storm to hit. Max never said much, but he did offer her his handkerchief whenever the tears started.

"Let's go home, Tillie," Ambrose said gently. "Mamma has sent the carriage for us and I hear they have prepared your favorite potato soup."

She hadn't eaten much and she knew the family was worried about her health now that a few days had passed.

"I don't mind walking, Ambrose," she said as she made her way toward the door. "I can meet you at home if you have other things to attend to and need the carriage."

Her brother shook his head.

"Go on ahead to the carriage," he said. "I will be there shortly."

Tillie wasn't in a mood to put up much of a fight anymore, so she simply nodded and walked to the waiting carriage.

The driver came down and helped her inside. She crawled through the door and took her seat, then froze.

Someone was already in the carriage with her and it wasn't one of her brothers, which she had originally assumed. The spicy, soapy scent hit her hard and she sucked in a breath.

"Alexander," she whispered and he looked up at her and removed his hat. The sad smile he gave her nearly broke her heart again, but she bit her lip.

"Matilda Andrews," he began, his voice scratchy and worn. "You have ignored every message I've sent you these past 96 hours. Every. Single. One. Explain yourself."

She frowned at him.

"I have not received a single word from you the past four days," she replied. "Not a message. Not a note. And certainly not any of the answers I needed so badly the night I left. And if you were sending me *notes*, I can tell you now that my father would have burned them in the fireplace on the spot. Notes are for cowards."

A look of pain flashed in his eyes at the accusation.

"I will start with this: when I told you that I loved you, when I told you that you were mine and you were going to be my duchess very soon, I wasn't lying. Those words were, and are, still very much true," he said. "So no matter how angry you are, no matter the extensive amount of bodily damage your father and brothers have promised me should I hurt you again, we shall return to Warfield Manor and I am requesting a special license from the vicar to marry you this month."

He said the words with finality and crossed his arms.

"You are deluded," she said. "You think you can show up in my carriage and tell me what I am going to do with my life? If my father knew you were here, he would murder you with his own hands."

Alexander snorted at that.

"He *did* threaten to remove my head from my body if I ever hurt you again once I had explained everything to him," Alexander said. "But who do you think sent me here in *your* carriage?"

Her father, she thought with a bitter laugh.

"So explain," she said, knowing her father would have required an explanation himself.

That got a small smile from him.

"First, Eliza Masters is never welcome in our home again," he said. "She practically launched herself at me when I arrived in the room that night looking for you and would not stop to explain the reason for her tears. What you walked in on was just as confusing for me as it was for you and I had one arm around the back of her shoulders to keep the two of us from falling off the sofa to the floor, which would have been even more difficult to explain."

She searched his eyes and found the truth. Taking in a deep breath she finally nodded.

"It seems the Duke she'd been pursuing since breaking things off with me announced his engagement the night of the party," Alexander explained. "The current guess is that she was hoping to be caught by you so that you would break off our engagement and free me up for a second snaring in her net, though I dare say from that frightening way you reacted, Eliza Masters is terrified of you."

Tillie frowned.

"I didn't do anything," she protested and Alexander laughed quietly.

"No, but that emotionless, deadly tone you spoke to me in was a thing of nightmares that I think will take years to get over."

That cracked a small smile from Tillie, which must have encouraged him.

"And the bloody man — literally, the bloody man..."

She steadied herself.

"Unfortunately, he died the next morning, which was why I was unable to come to you immediately," he said. "He was a friend of the man you might have seen pacing in the background, Lord Bradley Hainsworth, Duke of Carrington. Carrington is an old school friend of mine and a true friend, to be sure. They had just returned from France together and from what I can piece of the story, they were betrayed by someone close to them."

How awful, Tillie thought. The poor man had been in so much pain. And his friend had been so distraught.

"Why could you not tell me any of this when I asked?"

Alexander moved forward and captured her hands in his, his eyes searching hers.

"I did not understand what was going on myself," he said. "I do not know what Bradley is into these days and who he is associating himself with. Suffice to say there are characters in his past that I would not want within ten city blocks of you and if I told you too much of what was going on, if you saw anything you were not supposed to see, I may not have been able to protect you."

She took in a deep breath and met his eyes. They were burning into hers, despite the dark shadows beneath them.

It looked like he had been sleeping about as poorly as she had.

"So it's that simple, is it?" She was teasing him now. "You just steal my father's carriage, tell me what I want to hear, and take me home?"

He nodded.

"If by home, you mean our home, then yes, Matilda," he said, pressing a kiss to her lips. "It is that simple."

Her heart fluttered at the contact.

"I suppose that's good then," she said. "It is already complicated enough between us."

He laughed and pulled her onto his lap so he could wrap his arms around her waist.

"Back to the Andrews home, Charles," he yelled out the window to the driver.

She giggled as he squeezed her tighter into him.

"But to be clear, Alexander, I will not be ordered about. Ask me nicely and perhaps I will agree to marry you," she told him.

He grinned. "I love that saucy mouth." He planted another kiss on it, before doing his best to kneel in front of her within the confines of the carriage.

"Matilda Olive Andrews," he said, looking up at her, "Will you marry me?"

"Absolutely, on one condition," she said. "You will never repeat the name Olive again."

"Agreed, love," he said, and seated himself next to her once again, pulling her tight towards him.

"Do not ever run off like that again, Tillie," Alexander whispered into her neck as he placed gentle kisses along her skin. "If you try, I'm going to have to tie you to my bed and keep you there permanently."

That got a laugh out of her.

"Is that a challenge, my lord?"

He nipped her neck again and pulled her hard against his chest.

"It is, my love," he said, turning her in his arms for a deeper kiss. "Try to run from me again and you'll be kept naked in my bed forever."

The very thought thrilled her and must have been evident in her expression because Alexander gave a pained groan.

"You'll be the death of me, Matilda," he said as he leaned her back against the cushions to show her how much he loved her She moaned at the contact and moved against him as he claimed her mouth in a scorching kiss.

EPILOGUE

The wedding was grand. Grander than any affair in recent memory in the village of Warfield and the residents never recalled seeing a more resplendent bride or a happier groom.

Tillie had been overjoyed when the day before the wedding, Tabitha and Nicholas had arrived at the manor. She hadn't thought they would be able to make it, and when she heard who had been announced, she ran through the halls to the home's entrance, launching herself at her best friend.

"I have so much to tell you!" Tillie said.

"And I you," Tabitha replied, as Tillie took in the large bump of her stomach.

"Oh Tabitha, you are expecting! You never told me in your letters."

"I wanted to tell you myself," she said. "Tillie, could you have ever imagined that the two of us would be married to dukes, and cousins?"

"Never in my life," said Tillie, laughing.

"I thought you and Alexander had a penchant for one

another at our wedding," said Tabitha. "I'm so glad you finally figured it out and got together."

"It has been quite the journey," responded Tillie. "Come, get settled in your rooms and I will tell you all about it."

They had spent the entire afternoon catching up with one another, and putting the last-minute touches on the wedding garments.

The ceremony was beautiful. Tillie's large family was in attendance of course, all of her brothers lined in the front pew, shooting Alexander looks that promised if he didn't take good care of their sister, he would have the seven of them to answer to. Alexander, however, had eyes only for his bride.

Tillie had never looked more beautiful. She had left much of her hair down around her shoulders, where it curled softly around her face. She had designed her dress herself, of course. It was a pale-yellow gown, the lace bodice accentuating her curves, while the skirt flowed to the floor with a delicate train that trailed behind her down the aisle.

She had been surprised when her usual size didn't fit once the dress was created, and she had to let it out a little in the back.

How silly she had been to resist marriage all her life. It wasn't marriage itself that was imprisoning, she realized, it was the marriage to the wrong person. She had found her prince charming, however, and she felt freer than she ever had before.

She was still coming to terms with the fact that she was now a duchess. She was pleased that Alexander preferred to spend about half the year in London. She would be able to keep up with the latest fashions. Alexander was more than happy to support her dressmaking enterprises, and in fact encouraged her to continue.

He knew too many women of the peerage who idled their days away with gossip and chatter, as they had no greater purpose in life. While he wasn't an expert in fashions of the day, he was aware that she had a great talent that he didn't want to see squandered. He also suggested that Tillie begin attaching her name to her designs. He felt she deserved to be celebrated for her talent.

There were whispers among the guests that the bride seemed a little rounder in the middle than she perhaps had been at the holiday festivities three months prior, but those little whispers were quashed by cheers and well wishes as the bride and groom rode away in their carriage, making their way back to the manor as Duke and Duchess.

The house was louder and fuller than it had been in quite some time. Tillie felt like she was back at home, and, as much as Alexander enjoyed a quiet moment to themselves now and again, it felt like the house had finally come to life. It was Tillie who had done that, and he looked forward to filling the house with light and laughter as the two of them made it their home together.

"You are radiant," Alexander said for the tenth time since he had seen her at the back of the chapel, on her father's arm.

"I should hope so," she laughed and shook her head at his confusion. With a sigh, she put her hand over his and pressed a kiss to his lips.

"I am expecting, Alexander," she whispered against his mouth and closed her eyes, almost worried about his reaction.

"You are sure?" His voice was shaking but the smile she saw when she finally looked up had split his face from ear to ear.

"Very sure," she said. "But I didn't want to jinx it and thought it might make a good wedding gift to you?"

She was uncertain, but the look of joy on his face confirmed what she had hoped — that Alexander was thrilled at the idea of a family with Tillie.

"You're irresistible," he said, his hands on her body and his mouth all over hers. "If this is what pregnancy looks like on you, we'll end up with a brood of children in no time, my love."

The carriage rolled toward Warfield Manor where a new life, literally and figuratively, awaited the Duke and Duchess of Barre — a new life where they would live happily for now and forever.

~

THE END

~

Sign-up for Ellie's email list and "Unmasking a Duke," a regency romance, will come straight to your inbox — free!

www.prairielilypress.com/ellies-newsletter/

You will also receive links to giveaways, sales, updates, launch information, promos, and the newest recommended reads.

ONCE UPON A DUKE'S DREAM

HAPPILY EVER AFTER BOOK 3

PREVIEW

the next in the series, the story of Bradley and Isabella...

PROLOGUE

Bradley flicked the reins of his horse, pushing him to run even faster as the large manor came into sight. He looked at the horse keeping time beside him, and didn't like the look of the man who was thrown over the saddle. Roger didn't move, but the light rise and fall of his chest that gave Bradley a bit of hope.

His heart pounding nearly in time with the rhythm of the horse's hooves, Bradley Hainsworth, Duke of Carrington, raced the horses up the drive, but went around the back of the palatial manor house to the servant's entrance, as was fitting the situation. He vaulted off his horse, ran to the house and pounded loudly until finally a servant opened the door, an incredulous look on his face as he took in Bradley's blood-stained shirt, windswept hair and the crazed look in his eye.

"Are you here for the house party? I believe, sir, you may have the wrong entrance..."

While the man clearly didn't know who he was, he had seemed to discern from his dress that he was not a man that belonged at the servant's entrance. Bradley, however, had no time for explanations.

"My friend is gravely injured. Send for the physician at once, and find a man to help me bring him inside to a place he can be treated," Bradley commanded.

As the man began walking away, Bradley called out after him, "Oh! And find Alexander Landon, Duke of Barre!"

The man recognized his words with a slight nod of his head. He had likely already been on his way to find the master of the house.

Bradley helped carry Roger inside, placing him on a small couch in a room in the servant's quarters that was clean and comfortable enough. He helped the servants who began bustling about, tearing away Roger's shirt, and he grimaced at the hole the bullet had made in his friend's chest.

Their old friend the Duke of Barre finally appeared in the doorway, his face aghast as he took in what was in front of him.

"My God, Carrington! What in the…?"

"I've not much time to explain, but I was helping Roger escape from France, where he had been falsely imprisoned. We were on our way back to England when we were ambushed," Bradley said in a rush. "I must apologize for imposing on you like this, but we were so close to Warfield and I didn't know where else to go."

"It's fine," Alexander replied. "I'm glad you felt you could trust me."

A servant called to Alexander from the doorway, and he turned to Bradley. "I'll return shortly," he said. "The physician should be here momentarily."

Bradley nodded, and now that he had time to consider

all that had happened, guilt began to descend onto his shoulders. All that had happened was his own fault.

He recalled the day he had agreed to help the Foreign Office with their request. They could not infiltrate the highest ranks of society without drawing attention to themselves, but they were concerned that there were gentlemen who were passing on information to the French. Of course, there were more than a few Frenchmen within society, although every one of them made it more than clear that their allegiance was with the English. They had all lived in England for some time and had not returned to France in a number of years, meaning that suspicion about their loyalty was not often questioned. Bradley had agreed to assist the Foreign Office in watching such gentlemen, but, until his trip to Paris, nothing had been of note.

Roger had been eager to help, and volunteered to travel to Paris to see what he could discover.

Bradley realized that someone knew who they were and what they were doing for the Foreign Office, although he did not know how they had discovered such things. Perhaps Roger had let it slip, although that was highly doubtful given how trusted a friend he had been. Regardless, Roger's capture and imprisonment in France had led to Bradley traveling to the continent to help his friend return to England, and things had only grown more complicated from there.

There had been strange circumstances that had placed Roger under guard in the first instance, for his friend had been arrested for stealing, despite the fact he would never have pilfered a single thing. Bradley knew Roger, the son of an earl and his boyhood friend, better than anyone.

Roger had been shaken by what had occurred, telling

Bradley over and over that he had not stolen anything. Bradley had been so concerned with fighting his friend's cause and getting him out from behind bars that he had given very little thought to the bizarre nature in which Roger had been imprisoned.

Now that he thought of it, the fact that his friend had been arrested while out walking the streets of Paris had been strange indeed. Even more so the fact that stolen items were apparently recovered from his apartment, although Roger had stated over and over that he had never seen such things before. Regardless, Bradley had used his power and title to remove Roger from prison, although they had been strictly instructed to remain in Paris until matters were settled within the courts – but Bradley had insisted that they leave at once.

He and Roger managed to make their way to England's shores without too much difficulty and relief had filled them as they'd begun their ride back to London. That reprieve had been shattered in an instant when Roger had been thrown backward as a bullet struck him in the chest.

The servants continued to clean the wound the best they could, and soon there was a large pile of bloody bandages in the corner of the room. Bradley paced back and forth in front of the window. It had felt like they had been here forever, although truly it had not been that long.

"Where is the doctor?" he inquired. "And where did Barre disappear to? We need him!"

"Your Grace," one of the valets spoke up. "The Duke's fiancée called him and he went to assist her momentarily. He should return at any moment."

Bradley nodded and resumed pacing.

The physician finally did appear, and it took no more

than a quick look at Roger before he turned to Bradley and slowly shook his head. "There's nothing I can do."

Bradley had been outraged, and despaired for his old friend. He sat by him all night, praying for life to return to his body. But the physician had been right. Come morning, Roger took his last breath.

1

"Stop! No!"

Bradley Hainsworth, Duke of Carrington, woke with a start, hearing his words echoing around the room. Breathing heavily, he stared at the fire in the grate, trying his best to calm his frantically beating heart.

"It was just a dream," he muttered to himself, passing a hand over his face and feeling the sweat on his brow. His skin was gooseflesh, his breathing ragged. "It was just a dream."

However, the truth was that it was not just a dream. It had actually happened, and the memory simply would not leave him. It was there every night, each time his head touched the pillow, repeating itself over and over again.

Roger was dead.

Bradley could still hear the gunshot, could still see the blood-soaked shirt as his friend took his last breath. The blame for all of it sat firmly on his shoulders.

Rubbing one hand down his face, Bradley pushed back the covers, made his way to the window and threw open the drapes, drinking in the early morning light. He could not go back to sleep now, not when the memories of his friend continued to haunt him.

"I will find the man responsible," he bit out, his breath steaming up the glass in the window. "I swear to you, Roger, justice will be done."

Leaning his head against the cool glass, Bradley closed his eyes for a moment, feeling the heavy burden of duty once more roll onto his shoulders. It was not he who had shot Roger, although he could understand why it certainly looked that way. After all, it had only been him and Roger on the road back to London, having made their escape from France.

Groaning to himself, Bradley left the window in order to ring the bell. It was early yet, but he needed something in his belly and certainly some coffee if he was not to spend the entire day yawning. Unfortunately, he had a ball to attend this evening, which meant that he would have to be washed, dressed and prepared for such an event.

It was not that he didn't appreciate the invitation, only that he knew that his title and the fact that he remained unattached were the sole reasons for him to garner so much attention from the rest of society. Doubtless, there would be various ladies with their eyes on him, and he would be introduced to countless debutantes with their fawning mamas behind them.

No one cared for *him*, they only cared about his title and his wealth. Most men seemed amenable to finding themselves in such a situation, for they quite enjoyed the attentions of so many pretty ladies, but he could not confess the same. The more they tried to cling to him, the more he withdrew, but that did not mean they relented. It was as if they saw him as a challenge, like it was all a game. They wanted to see which of the young ladies would claim his attentions, and then all of society would be abuzz with the news.

Sighing heavily, Bradley walked over to the fire, finding the room a little chilly. The maid would be in shortly to stoke it, but there was no reason he couldn't do such a thing himself. Adding a few logs and some coal to the grate, he watched in satisfaction as the flames caught almost at once, bringing a wave of heat toward him. Tugging a blanket from his bed, he swung it around himself, fully aware that he now looked like something of a wraith. There would be no more sleep for him tonight.

At that very moment, the door opened and a pale-faced maid poked her head in, apparently surprised to see him awake so early.

"Your Grace," she stammered, not quite looking at him. "I have your breakfast tray."

"Enter," he muttered, glad that the blanket was still draped about him so as to cover his bare feet. The maid placed the tray down by the fire, her eyes darting around the room.

"Send the valet up in about half an hour, will you please?" Bradley asked, dismissing her. The aroma of freshly buttered toast and hot coffee was already making his stomach growl, and as soon as the door closed, he sat down at once and began to eat. However, his mind still remained full of thoughts of Roger and the unknown killer. Would he meet him at the ball this evening, entirely unaware of what the man had done? How could he determine which was the man he was looking for?

"ARE you sure you're ready for this?"

Bradley let out a breath, sending his friend a wry grin in response to his question. Alastair sat slouched in an upholstered chair across the room, one foot swinging lazily over the arm. He had grown tired of waiting for Bradley downstairs, and so had come to determine what was taking so long. His friend was stalling, as always, putting off their inevitable entrance to the ball. "Can you tell just how much I am looking forward to this evening's entertainment?" Bradley asked.

Alistair, Earl of Kenley, was always up for a social event, and he shot him a sharp look. "You don't look particularly convincing, Carrington."

Taking another deep breath, Bradley tried to settle his shoulders, pushing away the tension he felt. He was grateful that Alastair had been willing to come to London to assist him, glad that he had at least one more friend he could rely on. Of course, it had meant telling Alastair everything but, once the cards were on the table, Alastair had been just as keen as he was to unmask Roger's killer.

"It may be dangerous," Bradley had warned, only for Alastair to laugh.

"It is not as though I am so tied up in business that I cannot spare a few weeks," Alastair had replied, shaking his head at Bradley. "Come now, do not worry about me. You are quite right to decide that you cannot face this alone. I am determined to help you."

"It is just as well," Bradley muttered regarding his thoughts on the evening's entertainment, as he took one final look at his cravat. "It seems I am something of a bore these days and no one else wants to particularly keep me company."

Alastair chuckled. "You've always been a bore, Carrington, but I believe it suits you. There is a certain dignity about you that draws the ladies to you regardless of how grumpy you look."

Rolling his eyes, Bradley sighed dramatically. "It is my curse to bear."

"If you were only not so handsome," Alastair sighed, shaking his head in mock envy at his friend's dark good looks, although his own striking face and blond curls were equally as pleasing to the ladies. "Or if you did not bear such a high title, then I am quite sure no one would be interested in you."

Bradley could not help but chuckle. "How unfortunate for me, indeed."

"Have you actually any intention of taking a wife?"

The serious question had Bradley frown. "No, indeed. Not in the least, at the moment, although it does not stop the grasping mamas from sending their daughters toward me!"

"You are going to have to marry at some point."

Bradley grimaced. "Yes, I am fully aware of that, but I feel as though I cannot allow myself such pleasures until Roger's killer is brought to justice." He could feel Alastair's eyes on him, and hoped his friend understood. It was a blessing that Alastair had offered to assist him in looking into the matter, when, in truth, Bradley had very few close friends and even fewer that he could be entirely honest with.

"I understand," Alastair said, slowly. "Then I shall simply have to do your share of dancing as well as my own."

Relieved that the atmosphere lightened once again, Bradley chuckled. Alastair had always been able to attract a great number of ladies. Bradley thought that it must have something to do with Alastair's ability to put almost everyone at ease and say the exact words every lady wanted to hear, accompanied by that charming grin of his.

"Very good, Kenley," he muttered, finally satisfied with the state of his cravat. "Come then, we should go."

Once Upon a Duke's Dream is now available for purchase on Amazon and to read free in Kindle Unlimited!

ALSO BY ELLIE ST. CLAIR

Standalone

Unmasking a Duke

Christmastide with His Countess

Her Christmas Wish

Happily Ever After

The Duke She Wished For

Someday Her Duke Will Come

Once Upon a Duke's Dream

He's a Duke, But I Love Him

Loved by the Viscount

Because the Earl Loved Me

Happily Ever After Box Set Books 1-3

Happily Ever After Box Set Books 4-6

Searching Hearts

Duke of Christmas

Quest of Honor

Clue of Affection

Hearts of Trust

Hope of Romance

Promise of Redemption

Searching Hearts Box Set (Books 1-5)

The Unconventional Ladies

Lady of Mystery

Lady of Fortune

Lady of Providence

Lady of Charade

Blooming Brides

A Duke for Daisy

A Marquess for Marigold

An Earl for Iris

A Viscount for Violet

ABOUT THE AUTHOR

Ellie has always loved reading, writing, and history. For many years she has written short stories, non-fiction, and has worked on her true love and passion -- romance novels.

In every era there is the chance for romance, and Ellie enjoys exploring many different time periods, cultures, and geographic locations. No matter when or where, love can always prevail. She has a particular soft spot for the bad boys of history, and loves a strong heroine in her stories.

She enjoys walks under the stars with her own prince charming, as well as spending time at the lake with her children, and running with her Husky/Border Collie cross.

www.prairielilypress.com/ellie-st-clair
ellie@prairielilypress.com

Printed in Great Britain
by Amazon